THE INNOCENT REBEL

Also by J. E. Ribbey

The Last Patriots Series
American post-apocalyptic thrillers
Fall of Freedom
Archangel
For You, My Dove
Rise of the Eagle
Operation Gray Owl

Young American Adventures
Middle grade historical fiction
The Innocent Rebel
Defiant Retreat
Under the Wing of the Storm
Deceptive Victory
A Mending Wound
A Traitorous Hero
Final Hope
Dangerous Love

Scan the QR Code or visit
https://store.jeribbey.com/
to find your next book!

The Innocent
REBEL

by J. E. RIBBEY

Soraya Jubilee PRESS

SORAYA JUBILEE PRESS
An imprint of The Jubilee Homestead LLC,
Stanchfield, Minnesota

Copyright © 2023 Joel and Esther Ribbey

Visit the author's website at JERibbey.com

All rights reserved. No parts of this publication may be reproduced, stored in a retrieval system, or transmitted in any form or by any means, electronic, mechanical, photocopying, recording, or otherwise, without the prior written permission of the copyright owner.

Printed in the United States of America

LIBRARY OF CONGRESS CONTROL NUMBER: 2023900167

Print ISBN: 979-8-9875823-0-5
eBook ISBN: 979-8-9875823-1-2

Edited by Holly Crashaw
Cover design by Esther Ribbey

This is a work of fiction. Any similarity between the characters and situations within its pages and places or persons, living or dead, is unintentional and co-incidental.

To our own four young adventurers.

Chapter 1

April 18, 1775

Papa was called to a meeting late tonight. A strange rider came galloping through town raising all kinds of alarm, saying, "The British are coming, the British are coming!" When Papa returned, I heard him moving about, gathering his hunting supplies and other things. I'm not sure what. It was odd, though, Papa's feet shuffling heavily on the floor as though his legs were difficult to raise. Papa's never been one to drag his feet.

People in town have been murmuring for a while now about a war coming. Fights have even broken out in the tavern over it. Papa doesn't say much about it, though his eyes have seemed more distant and contemplative lately. I think he is afraid. Since Mama died, all we have is him.

My brothers, Benjamin, Abe, and David are a handful, and that's why Papa is so blessed to have me. It takes a good, strong girl *with an even temperament and near-perfect moral discretion to rein in such mischievous and whimsical[1] sacks of masculinity. Though it is my cross to bear, I know Mama would want me to do my best and help Papa in any way I can. I wish she were here. Papa could really use her love tonight.*

My candle is all but gone out, and Papa has been quiet for a bit. Hopefully tomorrow will be a brighter day. Goodnight.

Mercy Young, 12 years old.

The eastern horizon was just turning grey when the clanging church bell sent Mercy bursting from her blankets. Her tiny room was dark except for a faint shaft of light that filtered through the crack of her door. The muffled sounds of shouting voices and tromping feet came through her window. Some were easy to recognize. Lexington, after all, was a small community, the kind where everybody knows everybody, and everybody knows everybody's business.

Just then, Mercy heard knocking at their front door. Widening her door open ever-so-slightly, Mercy could see a couple of men talking with her papa. One was Nathan Smith,

---

[1] You can find the definition for this and other uncommon or difficult words in the glossary at the back of the book.

the blacksmith, and the other she couldn't quite make out. Speaking in hushed tones, the men fidgeted about uneasily, holding their muskets.

Muskets! Mercy thought. *Why would they be holding muskets?!* Mercy's ears strained to catch their words. The men talked about British troops marching up the road, something about the militia, and that it was time to take a stand.

With that, the men left, and her papa turned. As he stared into the candlelight, his back leaning against the closed door, a somber expression spread across his face. He slowly glanced at each of his sons laying in their bunks across the open room, their eyes wide with both fear and excitement. Then his eyes met hers.

Mercy slammed her door, heart racing as she put all the pieces together. *Not this day!* The rider yelling the British are coming, her papa preparing his musket, the bell in the night, the shouting outside, and the men at the door. *The Militia was being called up. Papa was going to war.*

There was a soft knock. "Mercy?"

She shifted away from the door, allowing her father to open it. She could hear him step inside her little room, though she didn't want to face him.

"Mercy?" he asked again.

Slowly, she turned to face him, but as their eyes met, the tears she had been holding back broke loose and she began to sob.

"Papa!" she cried, falling into him. Her father's strong arms held her tight, and he kissed the top of her head.

"Mercy, I'm only going to the green with the men of the town," he reassured her. "I want you and the boys to stay inside today. Keep the door locked and stay away from the windows."

"What if something happens to you, Papa?" Mercy asked, wiping a tear from her cheek.

Taking her head in his hands, he said, "The Lord is always with you, Mercy. Never be afraid. He's the calm in the storm, and He's the morning light. Whom have we to fear with a God like that?"

His words were tender, but sure, and Mercy wished she could remain there in that moment forever. But with a final peck on the head, her father turned, and after assuring each of the boys, he walked out the door.

Mercy raced to her window and watched her father stride across the green through the clouded glass panes. The house was silent, not even David, the youngest, had stirred from where Papa had left him. A moment later, Mercy's thirteen-year-old brother, Benjamin, got up and headed for the stove.

"I guess we may as well get some breakfast," he said. "Abe, please fetch some water from the well. Dave, collect some eggs, and Mercy, fetch the pan. I'll go get some bacon from the smokehouse. Papa doesn't want us lingerin' out of doors for too long, so make it quick."

The family flew into action, glad for the distraction. At the stove, Mercy donned her apron and began working the fry pan with all the grace of her mother. She had died of the fever when David was only two, and Mercy had stepped up in a big way to mother them all, whether they wanted it or not. Papa had often told her that he would be lost without her, and Mercy couldn't agree more. By her estimation, they would all be naked and starving without her, and dumb as a rock to boot.

The door opened with a bang, and Abe staggered in with two water buckets sloshing against his legs.

"Did you see Papa out there?" Mercy asked him as he deposited his buckets in their place.

"No. There are too many men in the way. They all look more like Mr. Abrams did when he was waitin' for his baby to be born than soldiers."

"That's because they aren't soldiers," Benjamin interjected, handing Mercy the bacon. "Until today, they were just farmers and shopkeepers. You spilled water on the floor, Abe. Make sure you wipe it up."

At last, breakfast was all prepared, and just in time too, as Mercy could tell that David was about to gnaw his tongue with anticipation. Mercy brought the sizzling pan from the stove and dished up the eggs and bacon as everyone took their seats. Finally, Benjamin gave the blessing, and the younger boys dove in.

Mercy cut up her eggs and bacon properly and brought them to her mouth like a lady. She prided herself on being the only civilized member of the family. Benjamin stirred his breakfast around with his fork, glancing up at the window every now and again. Mercy knew he was thinking of Papa.

It was about the time they were wrapping up the dishes that they heard them, faint at first, but growing clearer by the second. Drums. Lots of drums. Thundering up the road toward Lexington. The younger boys paused their wrestling match as Benjamin and Mercy moved to the window.

Mercy held her breath as the drums thundered nearer and nearer. Then, at the spot where the road disappeared into the trees, a white horse appeared with a rider dressed in bright red. The rider was followed by an endless column of soldiers also dressed in red.

"They're here . . ." Mercy whispered breathlessly.

The younger boys leapt from the floor and started for the window, but Benjamin caught them and ordered that they all withdraw from the glass. Mercy knew that he was only following Papa's orders, and that it was for the best that the boys didn't see the army of red about to swallow the town green and everyone on it.

The drums shook the whole house with their banging. The windowpanes rattled in their frames. Then, all at once, it was silent, the kind of silence that causes a person to hold their breath for fear of breaking it. It was a long silence, a thick silence.

A loud voice barked a command and the army of red clanked and clattered into action, then another command and more clattering, then a third command. The strain became too much, and Benjamin got up from the table and moved to the window. Mercy went to follow, but he motioned with his hand for her to stay put and directed her with his eyes to comfort her wide-eyed brothers. Although she didn't like it, she obeyed.

A final command cut through the air, and the drums started again. Then another sound rang out, piercing the rhythmic din, a familiar sound, a musket shot. Mercy watched all the blood drain from her brother's face as the green exploded with violence. Benjamin dove to the floor as musket balls hammered the walls.

"Get down!" he yelled, pulling them to the floor.

All around them, men shouted, and muskets cracked. Wails of pain and fear, and the roar of angry orders rose above the chaos. It lasted only minutes, but they were terrible, long minutes.

The cadence of the drummers returned the green to order. The musket fire stopped, the tromping of soldiers died out, and the violence was subdued.

They lay on the floor in a trembling heap until a modest cadence drew the soldiers from the green, back onto the road, and carried them out of Lexington.

"Papa," Mercy whispered.

Chapter 2

As the last of the redcoats filtered out of town, everything was quiet—not even the birds sang. The caustic odor of sulfur permeated their little home. Mercy lifted her head from beneath Benjamin's arm, which he had wrapped protectively around them. As their eyes met, Benjamin released his hold on his family and sat back on the floor. He was still shaking.

As if on cue, a chorus of wails went up as the women of Lexington emerged from their homes to look for their husbands, fathers, brothers, and sons. Chills ran up Mercy's spine, and again she remembered—*Papa*. She jumped to her feet and ran for the door.

"Mercy, don't!" cried Benjamin.

But it was too late. Mercy stepped into the blinding light of the sun towards the green. As her eyes adjusted, she saw women she knew huddled here and there, caressing the heads of their fallen loved ones. Others combed the little field, looking helplessly for those who were missing. All of them were caught up in the dreadful chorus that reverberates from broken hearts when words have failed to do them justice.

Mercy's eyes darted here and there, frantically searching the field. She nearly jumped out of her shoes when a hand grabbed hers and spun her around.

"Mercy!" It was Benjamin. He looked at her sympathetically. Her younger brothers clung to him, looking scared and confused.

"We'll look for him together," he said at last.

With every victim who wasn't Papa, Mercy felt both a flicker of hope and then shame at rejoicing in someone else's misfortune. It took only moments to ascertain that Papa wasn't on the green. They searched around the other homes and buildings; they searched the ditch, the creek, and the woods. They found other men of the town and even helped some recover their dead and wounded. But there was no Papa.

Hours passed as they combed and re-combed the battlefield. Still, nothing.

"Ben, look!"

Mercy turned to see Abe tugging on Benjamin's arm and pointing at Mr. Smith, the blacksmith, and a couple of other men from town crossing the green at a trot.

Mercy felt her heart leap with hope inside her chest.

"Stay here," Benjamin commanded, setting off to intercept the men.

Mercy watched as Benjamin conversed with them. She did her level best to discern his expressions, but her interpretations led her down so many rabbit holes, she decided to give up the whole thing and wait. *Where could Papa be?*

After a few moments, Benjamin trotted back. His expression was somber, and he searched their eyes as if questioning whether or not he should divulge the information in the present company. At long last, he sighed and began.

"Papa's alive," he started.

Mercy's face lit up, but something was off. Benjamin didn't appear quite as satisfied with the news as she.

Benjamin swallowed hard. "Papa's with the redcoats. He's been captured," he finished, barely above a whisper. Looking intently at Mercy, he added, "We're alone."

Before Mercy could respond, he began again. "There's more. This battle was only the beginning of the war. Men from all over, farmers, other towns, are gathering to avenge the slaughter that has occurred here at Lexington. The men I talked to and many more are positioning themselves to ambush the redcoats as they return from Concord. There's going to be a lot more fighting."

Mercy put her arm around Abe, as much to steady herself as to comfort him. *Papa is captured?* She caught the panic rising from her gut and swallowed it back down.

"At least we know he's alive," she said, trying to sound hopeful. "Where will they take him?"

"Mr. Smith didn't know for certain, but he reckoned he'd probably be taken to Boston and placed in the prison ship," Benjamin replied, not lifting his eyes to meet hers.

"Then how do we get him back?" asked Abe.

"Win the war, I guess," answered Benjamin.

"How long will that take? Will Papa be home tonight?" asked David.

Mercy pulled her little brother close. "No, Dave, not tonight. Wars tend to take a little while."

Distant musket fire echoed down the road. It was sporadic, much less organized than the volleys from the morning.

"They're a coming!" yelled Mr. Smith from across the green. "Everyone back inside!"

Benjamin and Mercy herded the boys back into the house.

Cracking musket fire continued throughout the day, some shots ringing out closer than others. At first, Benjamin kept the family away from the windows, but as the day wore on, they each spent time looking and listening.

At one point, a group of forty or so redcoats marched back through town. They no longer looked confident, nor as professional as the army that had attacked that morning. These redcoats looked weary, their feet drug on the ground as they staggered along. Every musket shot caused them to flinch, and their heads swiveled around nervously. Some of them wore makeshift bandages, and a couple lay on a cart pulled by a horse.

As the soldiers reached the woods on the edge of town, the trees erupted in musket fire. The whole thing happened so suddenly that the four of them dropped to the floor out of instinct. Mercy rose to her knees and peered out the window just as the British troops made a feeble attempt to return fire. Then all was quiet again, and the redcoats continued up the road more nervous than ever, leaving their dead and wounded behind.

As Mercy watched, she couldn't help but feel sorry for them. They had been so proud to take the field that morning. By all appearances, they'd been invincible, and now, only hours later, they were so terrified they fled, leaving their comrades behind. Though she wanted to hate them for invading their town and taking her father, she couldn't help but see them as people just like her.

As the day wore to a close, the fighting stopped. The Youngs, along with some of the women from town, provided aid to the wounded redcoats who had been left behind. Not everyone in town felt they had any business aiding "the enemy", but Mercy supposed that was to be expected. The town had lost more than a few men, and who was to say that it wasn't the redcoats lying there who were responsible? Alas, it was their Christian duty to love their enemies, and Mercy hoped that perhaps her kindness here would help her Papa to be treated the same.

The small town had seen more loss and destruction that day than any of them could remember. Though the British had been driven back to Boston, there was little rejoicing. Grief seemed to permeate everything. Sarah, the blacksmith's wife, had offered to let the Youngs stay at their home that night. It was a kind gesture but, the truth of the matter was that the Smith home was no bigger than theirs, and it wouldn't be a very comfortable night's sleep anyway. Benjamin declined with the promise of figuring things out in the morning.

That night, Mercy crawled into bed, exhausted inside and out. They had eaten a meager supper of beans and potatoes, but besides the fact that the meal itself lacked anything that even slightly resembled flavor, none of them had been very hungry. Benjamin said he was too weary to figure out any plans that night, so they might as well get some rest and wait until morning. Blowing out her candle, Mercy said a prayer for Papa, wherever he may be.

As fatigue began to overtake her, she heard Benjamin's whisper at her door.

"Mercy. We're gonna get him back. I don't know how, but we have to get him back."

Chapter 3

Mercy awoke with a start. Her restless night had been filled with nightmarish dreams colliding with a hazy reality to the point where it was difficult to discern between the two. Stumbling from her room, she realized she was sore everywhere. At the table sat the two younger boys, Abe and David, already working a breakfast of eggs and bread.

"Where's Benjamin?"

"He went out a while ago after makin' breakfast. He said he was going to get some information, and that if we needed anything, to ask you," Abe announced proudly.

"Information for what?" asked Mercy.

"How on earth should I know, Mercy?" Abe replied, a little offended that his morning report had not sufficed.

Mercy shot him a sharp glance with her hands on her hips. She would not be dealing with any rebellions today. Abe got the message and went back to his eggs.

David let out an involuntary giggle and was met with his own fiery gaze.

Mercy walked over to the stove and grabbed the pan and a couple of eggs from the basket. Her hand shook as she moved the pan to the stove. Steadying her nerves, Mercy drew a deep breath. She had never lived a day without Papa. She decided that it would be better to focus on what Papa would want her to do rather than focus on Papa himself. He had been able to depend on her before, and she made up her mind not to let him down now. After all, what good would getting Papa back be if his family had descended into savagery while he was gone?

"You boys better finish quick. It's time you were in your primers," Mercy chided.

Abe's jaw almost hit the table. "Mercy, we don't need schoolin'; we're at war."

"Abraham Young! Do you think the world won't need education after the war is over? Do you think folks won't need to know how to read and write anymore? Shoot! I'll bet the reason we can't settle this whole affair through respectful debate is the fact that King George can't read."

"Well, if the king can't read, then what's the use in me learnin' it?" Abe fired back.

"Of all the ignorant things . . ." Mercy towered over her brother on her tippy toes. "Abraham Young, foolish fellow as you may be, you're still my brother, and I refuse to have you grow up ignorant," she finished through clenched teeth. "Besides, it's in the Bible."

Abe's face screwed up in preparation for a good comeback, then suddenly, he deflated like a tired-out balloon. It was difficult to counter the Bible. If there was one message the good reverend had driven home, it was the fear of God.

"Alright, Mercy. If it's in the Bible . . ." he surrendered.

"Everything alright?" Benjamin asked, surveying the scene from the doorway, clearly enjoying the engagement.

"Benjamin! And just where have you been all morning!" demanded Mercy.

"Collecting information. Didn't the boys tell you?"

"I did tell her, right before she started subdagating me," complained Abe.

Mercy spun towards him triumphantly. "Sub-JU-gating, Abe. And that's exactly what you'll get if you don't get an education!"

Benjamin cleared his throat. "I found out that the militias are coming together and are hoping to surround the British in Boston. That's where Mr. Smith and the rest of the men from town will be. No one seems to know for sure what happened to the men captured from the green, but the general consensus is that they are probably on a prison ship." Toeing the floor,

Benjamin continued. "Now, Mrs. Smith has offered to take us in . . ."

"I don't want to live at the Smiths," David whined.

"Well, they don't really have the means to take us all, so I think it would be best if the three of you went to live with the Smiths, and I'll follow the militia and look for Papa."

There was a painfully awkward pause as Mercy and the boys processed what he just said.

"You want to leave us?" asked Abe in disbelief.

"It's not like that! It's just . . . it'd be one less mouth to feed, and maybe I could help somehow."

"I can help too!" exclaimed David.

"I know you can, Dave, it's just—"

"Papa says I have an adventuresome spirit, so I'm coming with you," declared Abe matter-of-factly.

"Then it's all settled," agreed Mercy. "We're coming."

Benjamin stared at them in dismay. Opening his mouth to object, Mercy met him with a fearsome glare that clearly announced the discussion was over.

There was a knock at the door that made them all jump. Sarah Smith stepped into the room and greeted the Youngs. Her face looked tired, the kind of tired that comes from worry and emotions. Managing a smile, she told them that she was expecting them for dinner that evening and that she would have some beds made up for them by then.

Benjamin shot Mercy a worried glance, and she scrambled to find a good excuse.

"I was already fixed to make the boys' dinner tonight, Mrs. Smith. Would it be alright if we waited until dark?"

"Dark?" Mrs. Smith looked surprised.

"Yes, ma'am, that would give us more time to pack things up here proper," added Benjamin.

Mrs. Smith eyed them suspiciously, but she must have been too worn out to argue. "Fine, dark then." And with that, she walked out the door and back across the green.

Mercy let out a huge sigh. She felt bad about deceiving Mrs. Smith, but it couldn't be helped. They had made up their minds and, one way or another, they were going to save Papa.

The four of them spent the afternoon packing up the house and gathering supplies for what lie ahead. When it came time to lay out all their gear on the floor for a final inspection, it became evident they had no idea what they were in for. Benjamin had crafted four rudimentary frame packs out of flour sacks, some twine, and bits of tree limbs. The packs were crude, but on short notice, they would have to do.

Mercy made sure each of her brothers had a change of clothes and their primers; she had no intention of letting their education lapse while they were away. She packed herself a small mirror, a brush, and her diary, amongst other necessaries. The boys had gathered a hatchet, cordage, a knife each, a hone stone, a bit of flint, fishhooks, candles, and a canvas tent. They each took some bread, Benjamin and Abe carried two drum canteens, and they finished off each pack with a wool blanket bedroll.

As the sun dipped behind the hills to the west, the four siblings crept out of the house and into the night. The cool, moist air caused Mercy to cling to her wool cloak. Her heart thundered in her chest. *We're really doing it.*

Chapter 4

"Mercy, if we don't keep moving, we're still gonna be in sight of town by morning," scolded Benjamin.

Mercy scowled at him and continued to rub her feet, refusing to move from the boulder on which she sat. The night was dark, the moon providing only a faint glow. Truth be told, Mercy knew they had only been hiking for a couple of miles, but her feet were taking a terrible beating on account of her somewhat loose-fitting shoes and the general roughness of the road. Besides that, the limbs from her rucksack had nearly rubbed her shoulders raw. How could anyone expect a respectable woman like herself to continue on under such duress?

"We're never gonna rescue Papa at this rate," groaned Abe.

Sighing, Mercy returned her shoe to her foot and stood up. Straightening her dress, she said, "Alright, boys. I'm ready."

David took Mercy's hand for fear of the dark, but it was just what she needed to put on a stiff upper lip and trudge on.

As the four of them made their weary way towards Boston, Mercy had to admit that she had not been as prepared as she thought for this sort of adventure. The folks in the stories she'd read had failed to mention the immense fatigue and pain one has to endure to be a hero. At least she hoped they would be heroes.

After they had gone a few miles more, it was clear that neither Dave nor Mercy were going to make it all the way to Boston that night. Benjamin picked a somewhat secluded spot below a ledge near a small stream. He set Abe to work collecting tinder and branches while he and Mercy set up the tent. Without a lantern, the work was cumbersome, but at last, they were able to get things into place well enough. Abe had amassed a good-sized pile of branches, birch bark, and some dry grass.

"Well done, Abe," Benjamin exclaimed.

Together, they created a small ring with stones they found near the creek. Rubbing the grass together between his hands, Benjamin created a fine fluff that he turned into a nest. To this, he added some shavings of birch bark and, after placing the nest into the center of the ring, he pulled out a bit of flint. Holding the flint just above the nest, he struck it with the back of his knife three times in rapid succession. A shower of sparks landed in the nest and began to smolder. Benjamin carefully picked up the nest and blew gently on the ember.

Little by little, small threads of glowing orange crept across the nest until Benjamin added a final blow, causing the nest to erupt in flames. Everyone cheered as he placed it back in the center of the ring and added some more bark and small twigs to the fire.

"That's just how Papa would have done it," said Mercy, smiling.

The four of them huddled around the crackling fire and, as the warmth drove away the chill from their bones, fatigue took over. Benjamin insisted that Mercy and David take the tent, while he and Abe rolled out their blankets near the fire. Mercy gratefully took her place next to Dave on the hard ground, though she doubted she could sleep.

It wasn't until beams of morning light woke her that she realized just how tired she had been. If she thought she had been tired the day before, she was sadly mistaken. Mercy felt every lump and pebble she had slept on, as well as the pain in her feet and shoulders.

"OOWWEEE," Mercy groaned as she sat up. Crawling to the opening of the tent, she climbed out.

"Morning, Mercy."

Benjamin was working his own sore muscles while sitting next to the small fire. It was obvious he had not fared any better than she. As Mercy stood and stretched her limbs, an unusually satisfying sensation of pain and release rippled through her body. The feeling made her a little dizzy, and she caught the edge of the tent to steady herself.

Just then, Abe sat up in his blankets and declared he was near starvation. Mercy staggered over to his rucksack and, after a little rummaging, pulled out a small cast iron frypan and a block of bacon.

"When did that get in there?!" exclaimed Abe.

"Oh, while you were out filling the canteens, I noticed that your pack had a little room in it, especially once I removed the slingshot and tin of fishing hooks." Mercy smiled proudly.

"You what?!"

"Oh, don't worry, Abe. I found some extra room in Benjamin's pack, so I put them in there."

Abe and Benjamin stared at her in disbelief.

"No wonder my back was so sore!" cried Abe.

"Don't be such a baby, Abe. A man's got to do his part. Besides, you'll forget all about it once I get the bacon on."

Abe collapsed with a groan, pulling his blanket over his head.

Within a few minutes, the smell of crackling bacon did its work, and Abe emerged from his blankets in spite of his earlier protests. Mercy met him with a satisfied grin.

"See, I told ya you'd forget all about it."

"Is that bacon?!" exclaimed David from inside the tent.

His shaggy head appeared at the entrance. He took a long sniff and climbed out, wrapping himself in his blanket.

"It sure is, and you have Abe to thank for packing the pan and bacon all the way here."

"Thank you, Abe," David said cheerfully.

Abe managed a half-hearted smile.

Across the fire, Benjamin let out a soft chuckle, shaking his head.

Mercy was surgical. She had not only taken the field, but she had also cut off any means of retreat. Abe would be toting the fry pan for the foreseeable future.

When they were all finished with breakfast, the four of them packed up camp. Mercy beamed as Abe grudgingly slid the fry pan into his pack. Apart from sore muscles, and the fact that they were on the road to a war to fetch Papa, who was probably aboard a prison ship, with little or no plan at all, things were looking up.

On the road, David kept them all entertained, pointing out every interesting tree, rock, puddle, and creature they came across. The sun was shining brightly, which worked wonders to warm the weary travelers. Mercy's mind began to drift towards Boston and what they might find when they got there.

The sound of horse hooves and wagon wheels approaching quickened Mercy's pulse. Motioning his family to the side of the road, Benjamin stopped and waited as the horse crested the small rise they had just traversed. *Are they redcoats?* Mercy wondered.

A beautiful buckskin horse plodded over the hill, followed by a weathered wagon with an equally weathered older man sitting atop it. Mercy breathed a sigh of relief; she had seen enough redcoats in the last couple of days to last a lifetime. As the cart creaked alongside their tiny column, the man called for the horse to stop.

"What are four youths such as yourselves doing on the road to Boston alone?" the man asked, eying each of them.

Benjamin stepped forward and, using his manliest voice, told him they had family in Boston they were going to meet. At first, Mercy couldn't believe that Benjamin would tell a lie, but the more she thought about it, it wasn't exactly a lie at all. Papa was in Boston, or as best they knew he was, and seeing how he was the only family they had, Benjamin was actually telling the truth.

"You got folks in Boston, ya say? Well, it's fixin' to be a mighty dangerous place. The war's in Boston. Are you sure your folks would want you to come that way?" he asked, still looking dissatisfied with their story.

"We must!" insisted Mercy. "They're all the family we've got left!"

The man stroked the silver stubble on his chin. "Alright," he finally agreed. "Seems there's no deterring you. I'm heading that way with some supplies for the militia; how about you all save your feet and ride in the wagon? It's a might bumpy but if'n you don't mind that, I'd be happy to do your folks a favor an' take you."

"That would be heavenly," cried Mercy.

"Thank you, sir!" added Benjamin politely.

The four piled aboard, wedging themselves amongst the barrels and crates, and with a sharp crack of the reins, the wagon was moving again towards Boston. The man had told the truth—the ride was indeed bumpy. After the better part of an hour, the sound of distant musket fire mixed with cannons caused the horse to dance in its traces. As they crested a hill, there on the horizon lay the sparkling harbor and Boston.

Chapter 5

Mercy's hands trembled as the wagon began its descent down the hill. Her nerves had not forgotten the conflict in Lexington. She watched Benjamin flinch with each random musket shot. Her excitement for the adventure they were on was immediately replaced with dread as the illusion of its glory faded away. This was a war.

"I think it would be best for you to jump off here," said the man, drawing the cart to a stop. "Perhaps you can find information about your folks here, in Cambridge. I'm afraid no one is getting into Boston today."

More sporadic musket fire affirmed his suspicion. Benjamin nodded to the others, and they jumped from the wagon. Benjamin thanked the man and shook his hand.

"I hope you find who you're looking for," the driver said, and he pulled away.

Mercy looked around. The kind man had left them on the outskirts of Cambridge. It was not as grand a town as Boston, but it was a good town nonetheless. She had been there many times before, but it was different now. Everywhere, folks were nailing boards over their windows. Colonists with muskets roamed here and there, some running, some walking. Musket fire seemed to echo from every direction.

The people were also different from before, wide-eyed, with worry etched into their features. And the smell. Coastal towns always had their own queer sort of smell, a mixture of fish, the sea, and a general industrial odor. Now, there was something new—sulfur. That familiar smell from the green in Lexington, the smell of war. Presently, a cart carrying deceased militia men rolled past. Mercy felt her world begin to spin.

"Let's go, Mercy," Benjamin said, taking her by the arm and leading the three of them off the road. He led them past a white painted house with a sign hanging above the door: Physician's Office. A couple of men helped a comrade through the door, while several others were placed on makeshift cots on the lawn. There was a general disorder to the whole thing, making the entire situation most pitiful. Mercy felt herself beginning to slip again.

Just then, a woman's voice called out through the din, "Children, children! Get over here. What are the lot of you doing in the streets at a time like this?"

A round-faced woman, not more than five feet tall with kindly eyes, herded the four of them out of the street and through the rear entrance of a tavern. Even from the back room, the riotous behavior of the men in the tavern was most discomforting. The woman looked them over from head to toe, her eyes full of pity and kindness.

"Where are your folks?" she asked sweetly.

Before Benjamin could answer, Abe pointed out the window to the harbor, where a couple of British ships were at anchor. The woman furrowed her brow as though she didn't understand. Benjamin opened his mouth to respond, but the lady put up her hand to stop him and asked Abe, "Where exactly are your parents, child?"

Abe looked at the floor. "The regulars took Papa."

"And your mother?"

Abe kept his eyes on the floor and just shook his head.

"Oh, my Lord," the woman gasped. "You poor dears. Have you anyone else?"

"No, ma'am," answered Benjamin. "We came here to fetch him back," he said determinedly.

The woman's face turned to pity once more.

Just then, a man appeared in the doorway separating them from the tavern. He was a handsome man in his mid-thirties, Mercy guessed, and he looked plum worn out. Sweat stained his collar, his hair had fallen out of its keeper here and there, and his face glistened. He eyed them all briefly and then, looking at the woman, he sighed.

"Abigail, we need more ale. Water it down if you have to, but keep it coming. I fear what will happen if we turn them away."

Abigail nodded her understanding, and the man returned to the tavern. She immediately went to work, removing the top off a keg of ale. It was two-thirds empty. With a sigh, she grabbed a pail and headed out the door.

Mercy gave Benjamin a nudge. "Give her a hand, Ben."

Benjamin nodded, and shrugging off his pack, he followed Abigail out the door. A few minutes later, the two of them returned, Benjamin carrying the pail. She motioned for him to pour it into the keg, and so he did.

With a sorrowful smile, she explained. "We have to fill it all the way to the top."

Benjamin nodded and headed back out the door. Abe found another pail and followed him. It took no time at all, and the keg was full. Abigail filled a pitcher with the watered-down brew and hurried into the tavern. Mercy watched the woman work feverishly to keep up with demand.

As Abigail returned from her twentieth trip into the tavern, Mercy cut her off at the keg. She reached out and took the pitcher from the exhausted woman's hands and said, "Let me have a go for a while, ma'am." She reached to take the pitcher back, but Mercy had already turned her back and began filling it.

For the remainder of the day, the Youngs took turns helping Abigail and her husband, Henry. They worked for hours on end, until finally, at midnight, Henry was able to drive the remaining men from the tavern. Together, they finished cleaning up the aftermath the men had left behind. Mercy had never seen such a disgusting display in all her life, and had she had anything in her stomach, it surely would have come up. But as it were, the bacon they had eaten at breakfast was but a distant memory.

At long last, around one o'clock in the morning, the six of them sat around one of the tables by candlelight. They were exhausted, filthy, and emotionally spent.

"I don't know how we would have survived the day without your help," Abigail said. "We have an extra room you all are welcome to. It isn't large, but there's a bed."

"We haven't any way to pay you, ma'am, and we'd hate to be a bother," Benjamin replied. "We're used to sleepin' outdoors."

As tears began flowing down her face, Abigail shook her head. "You children have been such a blessing to Henry and myself. I don't know if the good Lord intended for you to bless us or for Henry and me to bless you, but we feel blessed all the same." With a quick glance at Henry, she continued. "We're unable to have our own children, though I've prayed for it every night for all these years. I'd like to think that if we had our own, they would be as fine as children as you all. And, if I had my own, I would hope that folks would treat my children with the kindness the good Lord has shown each of us. So, it'd be a blessing if you would share our house, even if it's just for a while."

"You said there's a bed?" queried David.

"Yes, child, and a goose down comforter to boot."

"Well, it's too late to do much more tonight anyway. I guess if it's alright, we'll take you up on the offer, at least for tonight," Benjamin said.

After washing up as best they could and downing a couple of hard-boiled eggs each, they turned in. The bed was only made for two, but Benjamin figured out how to make them all fit. He and Abe slept with their heads at the foot of the bed, while Mercy and David slept at the head. By staggering their bodies a little bit, they were able to make a halfway comfortable go of it.

Mercy was beyond exhaustion, and the bed felt so comforting that she was sound asleep before Benjamin had even blown out the candle.

Mercy awoke with a start, sitting upright into blinding sunlight. The distant report of a cannon rattled the glass in the small window. It had only been four days, and Mercy had already had her fill of war. Benjamin was already missing, along with Abe. Only she and David remained in bed. Downstairs, she could already hear Abigail working about the small kitchen, preparing for the day.

She gently shook her little brother. "David, it's time to get up."

David rolled over towards the window and let out a painful groan as he recoiled from the light. Mercy helped him out of bed and into his change of clothes. When the two of them reached the bottom of the stairs, Mercy saw Abigail floating around the kitchen, humming an old hymn. Her nose had a bit of flour on it, but her face seemed to glow with a sense of joy.

"Good morning, darlings," she said with a smile. "Have a seat at the table. I'll get you all fixed up with some eggs and biscuits, and you can wash it down with some fresh milk."

Mercy looked at the small clock hanging on the wall. It was 5:35 in the morning. She wondered if she would ever feel rested again. Mercy and David ate their breakfast in awe of Abigail, who seemed to never stop moving as she prepared for the day ahead.

As they finished their biscuits, Henry, Benjamin, and Abe arrived, rolling a couple of fresh kegs into the back room.

Henry wiped his brow and reported that at this rate, their stockpile of ale would run dry within the week.

"There are more men showing up every day, and they've got no means to live by," he complained. "We can't get supplies from the harbor anymore; the British aren't letting any trade take place. I was able to barter a few dozen eggs and some milk from the Douglas farm, and some flour from the store. I've got a bad feelin' things are gonna get scarce."

"The good Lord didn't bring us this far to fail us now, Henry," Abigail said, taking his hand in hers.

Mercy admired how she supported him, and took note that when they got Papa back, she'd do a better job of takin' care of him.

Henry's face softened. "Well, we're sure to make a fair bit before we run dry. Business has never been this good. I think we ought to water the ale down a bit to stretch it all the same. Those fellas get awfully surly when their cups run dry."

Abigail nodded her agreement. Turning to the Youngs, she asked, "Have you children made up your minds about what you're gonna do yet?"

Benjamin cleared his throat and looked at his siblings. "After talking with Mr. Henry this morning, I've decided..." He paused for a moment. "See, the thing is, it looks like it could be a little while before the British are whipped and, well, these folks could use some extra help on account of the militias and the war, and though we want to get Papa back right away . . . we really don't have the faintest notion how to go about it just yet. So, I reckon that this is as good a place as any to stay until we figure just what it is we're gonna do. If Mrs. Abigail is pleased to keep us, that is."

"We're not gonna get Papa back?" asked David fearfully.

Abigail knelt down and took his hand. "Of course, you're gonna get your papa back. It just might take a little while, that's all." Then she looked at Benjamin. "You're a fine young man, looking after your family. Your father would be proud."

"Well, if that's all settled," said Henry, "We'd better get to work. Lord knows it's gonna be another long day."

Abigail kissed David on the forehead and stood up. "Alright, Mercy, if you put on that clean apron over there, you can help me in the kitchen. Benjamin and Abe, if you'll help Henry in the tavern, that'd be a blessing. Mind your ears though, there's talk in there that'd make the devil blush. And David, if you'd be willing to run errands and fetch what's necessary when Mercy and I have need, I think we'll do a fine job of it."

By noon, it was obvious Henry had been right. The tavern had been filled to standing room only since ten o'clock, and fresh waves of men came and went like the tide. Mercy was so busy she hardly even noticed the sporadic musket fire and occasional boom of a cannon. It felt good to have a woman teaching her the fine arts of the kitchen again. She had apologized many times already for her shortcomings, but Abigail was patient, despite the urgent circumstances.

When the day finally drew to a close near midnight, all six of them rejoiced that tomorrow was Sunday and the tavern would be closed.

Chapter 6

June 16, 1775

The mood was somber in the tavern tonight. Most nights, the ruckus is so overpowering one has trouble putting her thoughts together. Benjamin said that he heard one of the militiamen mention a place called Bunker Hill. He said the militia were going to that hill during the night to take the high ground. The fighting has been nearly continuous since we arrived in Cambridge, but nothing like the fighting in Lexington. We've been at the tavern nine weeks now, and I can nearly run the kitchen by myself, except when it gets intolerably busy.

The contemptible speech and behavior of the militiamen has only steeled my resolve to defend what family I have left. I reckon that if one of these poor wretches were to darken the doorway of the church, he'd likely burst into flames. All that considered, I do say that while their manners are far from saintly, they do seem to possess a kinship all their own and a loyalty to liberty that is worthy of admiration.

It seems my cross to bear that I must contend with the allure of savagery laying siege to my brothers' impressionable minds from every side. I doubt there has ever been a woman on God's green earth who has been faced with a more difficult task. My only comfort has come from Mrs. Abigail, who seems just as keen on defending what little light may remain in those boys.

Why, it took a great deal of physical effort on both our parts to get David to take his bath, and we were forced to change the water twice on account of him falling headlong into the swamp while giggin' frogs. I fear there will be frightful disappointment when Papa returns if the war were to linger on for too long.

I miss Papa; I hope he is well, and I'm grateful that the weather is warm. He must be terribly lonely, and it must be frightening to be a prisoner in any place. I pray his captors will see his good heart and have compassion on him. Papa is a good man.

Mercy Young, 12 years old.

Mercy awoke with a sense of excitement. It was Saturday, which meant all she had to do was survive today and then tomorrow was Sunday. As their only day off, Sunday had quickly become the most anticipated day of the week.

Things at the tavern had quieted down some over the last few weeks, as the battle for Boston devolved into a stalemate. Abigail acquired a couple of used dresses for Mercy from a friend and even managed to find some clothes for the boys. The truth was, the tavern was beginning to feel like home, and Abigail and Henry were as good as family. It wasn't that they could ever replace Papa, but they had created their own place in Mercy's heart.

As Mercy reached the bottom of the stairs, Boston harbor erupted with cannon fire. The cannons echoed across the waters and slammed into the streets of Cambridge with thundering authority. The entire tavern shook. Immediately, everyone hit the floor. Then, one by one, Henry gathered them up and moved them all to the kitchen.

"Stay here!" he yelled over the din. "I'm gonna find out what they're shootin' at."

With that, Henry raced out the back door. He was only gone for a few moments.

"It's alright, they seem to be trying to level the hills above Charlestown peninsula, north of Boston."

The others moved to the windows in the tavern to look out over the bay. Plumes of earth and smoke rose from the distant hills with each cannonball. The ships in the harbor were shrouded in clouds of smoke as they unleashed their fury. On the peninsula, tiny specs fled from Charlestown towards the mainland. The ships' fervent assault paid the town little mind as it battered the heights.

Outside the tavern, militiamen marched here and there with their officers barking orders. The Cambridge townsfolk stopped the morning's work to take in the horrific spectacle. Then, all at once, the ships stopped firing. An eerie silence descended over the harbor. Mercy was half-shocked to see the hills on Charlestown peninsula still standing after such punishment, but there they were, looking none-the-worse for wear, except for a line of fresh earth extending across the crest of the hill she had not noticed during the barrage.

As the calm lingered, folks began to breathe and move about again. Somewhere, an axe began to chop wood, and a rooster crowed. People returned to their work, and the day seemed to thaw from its frozen state. In the tavern, Abigail threw up a prayer for the good folks of Charlestown and the boys up on the hills. She prayed for the British too, that they would have mercy on the rebels, and allow the colonies some liberty, and that the whole affair would just blow over. Then she prayed for Papa.

"I think it's over now. Folks are gonna start pouring in after a fright like that. I may even need a little ale to steady *my* nerves," said Henry.

That morning, the mood in the tavern was, again, different. The men spoke in hushed tones and there was a level of anxiety in their eyes that was difficult to miss. They took turns watching out the window, always looking towards the harbor. The feeling was eerie. Mercy couldn't believe it, but she found herself wishing the atmosphere would return to its usual rowdy self.

"What's the matter with everyone?" she asked Abigail.

"I'm not sure, but I think something dreadful has happened or is about to."

Henry and the boys joined them in the kitchen. "I think everyone should stay close to the tavern today," he said, placing a hand on David's shoulder. "Something's off, and those boys know it." He gestured with his head towards the tavern.

"Lord have mercy, what could it be, Henry?" asked Abigail.

"I'm not sure," said Henry. "But these boys are actin' like they're fixin' to meet the almighty. Not a one of them has asked for ale yet and it's nearly noon. Something tells me they're under orders."

The day seemed to drag on until a man yelled from the street, "Here they come!"

As if given an order, every man in the tavern gathered around the windows facing the harbor. Those who couldn't find room, ran out the door to watch from the yard. Benjamin and the boys headed upstairs to look out the bedroom window. Mercy looked up at Abigail.

"It's alright, Mercy, you can follow them."

In the bedroom, Benjamin had opened the window, and the three brothers were poking their heads out, chatting excitedly.

Mercy joined them and, following Abe's pointing finger, could see several small boats packed with redcoats rowing towards the hilly peninsula northwest of Boston. The ships in the harbor erupted again. Mercy pulled her head back inside after the boom of the first volley shook the house. Below them, the folks in the town went scurrying for cover and the militia moved to their positions. The smell of sulfur wafted through the town, its caustic odor signaling death.

As the redcoats formed up at the base of the hill, the cannon fire ceased. There must have been thousands of them standing in perfect formation, their red coats blazing, the sun glinting off their bayonets. A drum sounded, and the army began ascending the hill. As they neared the top of Breed's Hill, a sharp volley of musket fire halted their advance. The regulars opened fire with a volley of their own, and the battle was on. Continuous crackling musket fire and the hollers of men echoed across the bay. Mercy's pulse pounded. War was a terrible thing, and she could vividly imagine the scene unfolding on the hill.

After several minutes, the redcoats began retreating down the hill. The musket fire died down, only to be replaced by the thunder of cannons once more. Presently, there was a shout in the tavern below. It was Mr. Thomas, Dr. Morris's apprentice.

"Henry, we need your wagon and any ale you can spare, and if you have any bandages, bring those too! We've only a moment to evacuate the wounded from Breed's Hill!" Without waiting for a reply, he dashed away.

Next, it was Henry's turn to shout, "Mercy, Benjamin, Abe!"

The Youngs rushed down the stairs.

"Benjamin, Abe, fill every canteen you can find with ale. Mercy, help Abigail conjure up some bandages and meet me at the wagon quick as you can."

The Youngs flew to work and, within minutes, had gathered at Henry's flatbed wagon. As Henry finished lashing his team, the children piled their supplies behind the buckboard.

"Mercy, Ben, I may need your help with those wounded boys. Why don't you hop up here with me?"

They did as they were told. Abigail attempted to protest, but Henry's expression ended the conversation.

"Let's go, boys," he said with a clap of the reins.

The horses galloped down the road, their flanks rippling with each stride. The wagon jumped at every bump, forcing Mercy to throw her arms around Henry to keep from being thrown out. Out on the water, Mercy could see the ships still pounding away at the crest of the hill. If it weren't for the awful circumstances, Mercy would have been in rapture at their majestic appearance. As the wagon rounded the corner onto the Charlestown Neck, the ships ceased firing.

"Oh no," moaned Henry.

At the east base of the hill, the redcoats had reformed and were preparing a second assault. Henry snapped the reins again, urging the horses on. As they reached the opposite base of the hill, drums signaled that the regulars were beginning their march up. The horses strained against the braces as they climbed. Muskets clapped nearby and Mercy hid herself under Henry's arm while Benjamin clung to the buckboard beside her. Henry halted the horses just below the crest of the hill and a militiaman ran over.

"We're here for the wounded," Henry yelled.

The man nodded and ran toward the trenches, waving his arm to follow. Henry motioned for them to disembark, and the three of them started after him. The trench lay like a gaping wound at the narrow peak of the hill, with the ground falling gently away on either side. The men had piled all the dug-out dirt on the east side of the trench as added protection from the approaching redcoats. As Henry and the children neared, the militia let loose a deafening volley. Mercy clapped her hands to her ears, but it was too late. All around her, men yelled and dirt flew as musket balls glanced off the top of the trench several feet above their heads. Henry guided her towards the wounded men lying a few feet away.

"Mercy, give these boys some ale," Henry said, handing her a canteen.

Trembling, Mercy knelt down and removed the cork. Beside her, Henry and Benjamin made a makeshift stretcher by rolling a couple of short fence rails in the edges of a tarp. They placed the first man on the tarp, lifted him gently, and hurried down towards the wagon. Mercy fought through the panic of being alone and courageously moved from one man to another. Benjamin and Henry returned and, in seconds, headed off again.

The scene was complete chaos. Dirt rained down on her from above; her ears rang incessantly as muskets piled on insult to injury. Above her, pandemonium broke out as redcoats crested the berm. Mercy watched in horror as a grey-haired man was shot through the leg and fell into the trench beside her. She didn't have a moment to even think as the redcoat lowered his bayonet and prepared to descend on the fallen patriot. Rolling over the lip of the trench, she landed on the fallen man and spread herself over him.

Mercy closed her eyes and prepared for the pain that must come. There was a clash of metal and wood, the sounds of a violent struggle, the weight of a boot tripping over her sprawled body. Men shouted, her ears rang, her heart pounded, her body trembled; all in a moment that lasted a lifetime. Then the weight of a body fell over hers and everything was muffled. She was alive, she knew that, and as far as she could tell, she felt no pain. In the darkness of her closed eyes, she felt neither a part of the conflict nor separate.

At long last, the muffled cries around her faded, the musket fire ceased, and the body that lay on her was lifted.

"Mercy!" screamed a frantic voice. "Mercy!"

Strong arms lifted her from the ground and carried her swiftly away from the trench, away from the dark, away from the war. Opening her eyes, the day was bright, and she was forced to close them several times before she could focus. All motion ceased, and she looked up into the red tear-filled eyes of Henry. The relief swept across his face, and he broke. Henry pulled her close and sobbed. Holding her tightly, he kissed her cheek and forehead.

"I'm sorry. I'm so sorry. I'm sorry, Mercy. I'm so sorry, child." He gently set her on the back of the wagon between a couple of wounded militiamen. She sat up against the back of the buckboard and stared—it was all she could do. Henry and Benjamin climbed quickly onto the seat just as the man Mercy had jumped over was placed in the wagon, his head laying between her feet. Henry could wait no longer. He gently pulled the wagon around and, with all the care he could muster, guided it down the hill and onto the road.

As they headed towards Cambridge, Henry spent as much time looking back at Mercy as he did looking down the road. As she sat swaying with the wagon, a weathered hand reached up and took hers.

"Are you an angel?" whispered the grey-haired man. Though he was obviously in pain, his expression was kind and sincere.

Mercy managed a small smile and shook her head. "No, I'm just Mercy."

The man nodded his head gently and closed his eyes.

Chapter 7

When Mercy awoke, the room was dark. She could hear the usual ruckus in the tavern below. The sound was familiar and comforting. Her ears still rang, though the pitch wasn't quite so fierce. Her head throbbed like it had never throbbed before. Moving her hand to her head, she felt a damp rag.

Beside her, a chair creaked, and a woman's kind voice whispered, "Mercy, are you alright, child?"

It was Abigail.

"Do you need anything?"

"Water?" Mercy asked. She was desperately thirsty.

"Oh, yes, child. The good doctor said you'd be dehydrated, but otherwise you were in good shape and in need of a good rest. When Henry went to fetch him, he was adamant that he couldn't spare a moment. But when Henry told him the story of how you risked your life to save that poor man, he came right away."

Abigail rushed out the door and down the stairs to fetch water. *That poor man* . . . Mercy remembered the man being shot and nearly skewered, she remembered his hand taking hers, his kind eyes . . . *Did he live?*

When Abigail returned with the water, Mercy worked up the courage to ask. "Is that man alright? The one Mr. Henry told Doc about?"

Mercy braced for the answer. She didn't know him from Adam, but with all her heart, in this moment, she needed him to be alright. And if he weren't, she didn't know if she'd be able to bear it. In this war, this awful war, this war that took her father, she needed to know that there was still light somewhere in this horrible, tragic world of which she was now a part.

"Why, yes, Mercy, you saved him sure as I'm sittin' here! Henry told me the whole story of how the redcoats came over the rise and that man being shot. Henry saw the whole thing from the wagon. He saw the man fall and that redcoat fixin' to skewer him for sure. Then, he saw you roll into that awful ditch without a moment's hesitation and that redcoat pulled up short, just dumbfounded. Henry ran over to where you were and nearly beat that redcoat to death with a bit of fence rail. He said the redcoat fell right on top of you. When he brought you home, I swear, I've never seen Henry so frightened in all my life. He carried you up the stairs so gentle . . . Then he told me to stay with you. Didn't even take the time to explain and ran to fetch the doctor. About an hour ago, the doctor came by again to check on you. He told Henry you saved that man's life. He'll have a limp of course, but he'll keep the leg."

A wave of relief flooded over Mercy and crashed into the emotional exhaustion of the day. It then collided with the pounding in her head, overwhelming her defenses. It was all too much, and Mercy began to cry. Abigail joined her on the bed and wrapped her up in her arms, planting a soft kiss on her forehead.

"There, there, Mercy. You were a brave girl today—the bravest I've ever known. You did a powerful thing and witnessed something terrible. It's alright to cry."

She rocked her back and forth, gently stroking her hair. "You're alright now, girl, my brave girl."

After Mercy drank the water, Abigail fetched a fresh cool rag and insisted she get some sleep. The room went quiet again and Mercy slipped into a deep sleep.

The next day was Sunday and Mercy found herself being waited on hand and foot, as Henry insisted she was not to overexert herself. While David seemed to think it was fantastic to have a hero for a sister, Abe mumbled something about not understanding how trippin' into a hole and landing on an already wounded man made someone a hero. Even Benjamin was different. He hugged her more than once and did more than his share to make sure she was taken care of. When she had come down the stairs 'hat morning, he had rushed to meet her and with a firm embrace, he whispered, "I thought you were dead, Mercy."

She didn't feel like a hero. If she were being honest, she couldn't even rightly remember the events of that day very well. It was like trying to remember the dream you're having when you first wake up in the morning. At first, it all seems clear, but as the hours go by, you find it more and more difficult to remember exactly what happened. Another truth was, she didn't much want to remember. Every time she tried, the first thing to come back was the fear.

Later that day, she learned that, though the redcoats had taken an awful beating, the militia had lost the battle. The doc was once again swamped with wounded soldiers, and Mr. Hadley was the name of the man she had rescued. She attempted to thank Henry for coming to her rescue, but all he could reply was how sorry he was for bringing her up there and putting her in such danger. She didn't blame Henry. She couldn't. If it weren't for him taking her along, Mr. Hadley would have died, and that was the truth of it. After many attempts to convince him, Henry finally conceded and allowed that the Lord had a purpose in his foolishness that day.

As they began a new week, Mercy noticed that, although the militia had lost the battle, their spirits seemed to be higher than ever. The redcoats hadn't pressed farther inland and were still contained. Benjamin reported daily on the information he gleaned while working in the tavern. He had decided that it was divine providence that had prepared the way for them to take up residence in the absolute hub of militia gossip. It seemed that while the British were *contained* in Boston, they were not, however, cut off from supply. Ships from England continued to supply the soldiers in Boston in one fashion or another, while the militia had to depend on the locals for supply. And that supply was beginning to run out.

Tuesday afternoon, Abigail requested that the four of them make up some cane poles and do their best to fetch some fish from the ol' pond. The dwindling supplies in town had forced Abigail to come up with creative meals to serve at the tavern. In the camps, the militia were already living on a diet of beans and biscuits. Benjamin and Abe collected four canes and some twine, while David and Mercy scavenged worms from under old logs and rocks. When they had gathered a good amount, they met the boys at the pond.

Benjamin tied a six-foot length of twine to the end of each cane. The canes themselves were about ten feet long. At the end of the line, he tied a small hook, and two feet above that, he tied a bit of cork. They each hooked on a plump worm and extended the canes out over the water.

It was Dave who got the first bite. His cork bounced once, then again, and then all at once, it disappeared under the water.

"Get 'em, Dave!" yelled Abe.

Dave set the hook with a powerful yank that sent the poor creature blasting from the water. David fell backwards with the fish dangling above his head. They all burst out laughing, and Abe ran over to give him a hand. He no more than got the fish off the hook when Benjamin yelled, "Abe, you got one!"

Abe tossed the fish into David's lap and ran for his rod. He set the hook with a quick jerk and fought the fish out of the water, swinging it to shore. It was another fine panfish. Next was Mercy. She had just set her cane on a forked stick in order to help David with a new worm when her cork dove under the water.

"Ben, help Dave!" she shrieked as she set the hook.

"I can't!" yelled Benjamin. "I've got one too!" By this time, they were all laughing at the hysteria of the chaos.

Fish after fish they landed, bass and bluegill, crappie, and even a few catfish. Within an hour, they caught over thirty fish, laughed themselves sore, and, for the first time since Lexington, forgot all about the war. Mercy would never admit it to her brothers, but that day, she decided that perhaps not all things primitive were detestable after all.

By the looks of hunger on the militiamen's faces, they would likely have been robbed of their haul on the way back to the tavern had it not been for the respect they all had for Mercy. The tale of her bravery had spread through the camps and had even been embellished a little bit. Why, in one version, Mercy had supposedly killed that redcoat with her bare hands. Some of the men even nodded to her while she passed. The whole thing did make her feel terribly awkward.

At the tavern, Abigail declared them all heroes when she saw the bounty they had caught. She brought the fish into the kitchen and pulled a couple of long, slender knives from the rack.

"Mercy, could you give me a hand? This many fish is likely to take me all night," she said.

The boys washed up and headed into the tavern to help Henry, leaving Mercy to it. She picked up one of the knives and slid a beautiful bluegill off the line. She lay the still-wiggling fish on the cutting board. She hated this part. Abigail, noticing her hesitation, clubbed the fish for her with the pommel of her knife.

"There, child, it won't be feeling a thing anymore," she said, repeating the same courtesy on a panfish of her own.

It took three fish for Mercy to really get the hang of fileting, but by the time she was done, she was as good as one of the boys. She had done her level best not to look the poor creatures in the eye, but that's a difficult thing to do when the eye is so large and unblinking. Abigail didn't seem to have the same feelings for fish, or perhaps it was just that she couldn't afford to. The tavern needed ale and food to serve, and it was as simple as that.

Abigail showed Mercy how to batter the fish with flour and salt and fry them in the pan. The smell soon filled the tavern and set all their mouths to watering. Word must have spread after the militiamen had seen the children head to the tavern with all those fish. Even after cutting the filets small and serving them with heaping helpings of potatoes, the fish lasted less than an hour. Mercy doubted there were enough fish in the whole pond to feed the constant flow of men in the tavern, and she hadn't missed the look of concern on Henry's face when Abigail explained that they were almost out of potatoes.

That night, when the tavern was finally empty, Abigail surprised them with a plate of fish filets and potatoes she had set aside. Henry gave her an affirming smile and a peck on the cheek.

"It isn't good to muzzle the ox while it's threshing," she explained.

After Henry said grace, the Youngs took turns sharing the details of their fishing adventure and they laughed and ate until Abigail sent them all to bed.

Chapter 8

July 12, 1775

This afternoon, an elegantly dressed man rode into town astride a beautiful white horse. He sat tall in the saddle and wore a black hat on his head. He was as tall and broad as any man I ever saw and conducted himself with such decorum that he seemed dreadfully out of place in Cambridge. Benjamin heard the men in the tavern refer to him as General George Washington. They said he was sent by the Continental Congress to form the militias into an army. Benjamin also heard the men say the general was in a fury at the conditions in the militia camps and that starting tomorrow, things were gonna be different.

I do hope the general is a good man, and that he can help these poor devils find their way. Though their actions and words are often contemptible, I've found that I misjudged them. They are kind in their own way, and even sweet sometimes. They are full of humor, and though it gets to be a mite course once they've had an ale or two, they mean well. They are brave and loyal, and they love this land and freedom enough to die for it. Though they are far from perfect, my admiration for them grows by the day, and I hope the general comes to see them the way I do.

The boys and I have been kept busy with the work of the tavern. I've grown quite fond of fishing, as it has become a regular practice to provide meals for us to serve. Henry was able to secure good suppliers in New York for ale, beans, flour, and potatoes. He allows me to ride with him in the wagon when he goes for supplies, which provides a welcome change of scenery. Everywhere we go, folks talk of the war. Some are for it and others against. Henry taught me which merchants to tell that we were from Cambridge, and which to say we were from Boston.

We've still heard no word on Papa. I trust he is alright and pray every night that the Lord would watch over him. I wonder if he's heard the stories of the brave girl who saved a man's life. I hope he would be proud.

Mercy Young, 12 years old.

By mid-morning, the sweltering July heat had all the Youngs longing for a swim. It was only Thursday though, and the tavern still needed to be tended to. Benjamin was working the woodpile, as was his morning chore. Even at thirteen, he was quite handy with an axe, and Mercy stopped to give him a drink on her way back from the well. Sweat traced its way down his bare back as he gulped the water down.

"Think we can steal away for a swim this afternoon?" asked Mercy.

Benjamin handed her back the dipper and wiped his forehead. "I hope so. The sun seems mighty vengeful today. If you think it's hot for us, how do you think they feel?" Benjamin said, nodding to the militiamen drilling on the green.

Mercy looked to the green and the clumsy companies of militiamen marching in ragged blocks, making right turns, left turns, halting, and then doing it all again. On the far side of the green sat the general, stoic on his white horse, his aids at his side. Here and there amongst the companies, men barked orders and corrected those out of line. Another group of militiamen dug trenches, still others erected tents, all under the watchful eye of the general.

Mercy shook her head. "I'd better get this water in before Abigail comes lookin' for me."

The tavern was no escape from the heat. Abigail had propped open all the windows for a breeze, but there was no escaping it.

"Those poor dears," Abigail said as Mercy entered. "They're just as likely to drop dead from the heat as from the enemy on a day like today."

Mercy, seizing on Abigail's compassion, asked, "Do you think it would be alright if we took a swim this afternoon?"

Abigail hesitated before answering. She went into the storage room and reappeared with a fifty-pound sack of potatoes, then she brought out another.

"I'll make you a deal. If we can make it through peeling all these potatoes and there's still time before the supper rush, it's alright with me. I have a feeling that those who can afford it are gonna be mighty hungry after a day like today. We're likely to be swamped."

Mercy let out a determined sigh. "Deal."

She picked out a sharp paring knife and pulled up a chair. Taking the top potato out of the sack, she went to work with skillful vigor. The skins rolled off the potatoes as she carved, and within minutes, she had amassed a small pile of the ivory spuds.

"Slow down, child," chided Abigail. "You're likely to lose a finger if you keep that up."

Mercy just smiled and kept on peeling. She enjoyed getting a rise out of Abigail. "It's going to take more than a sack of potatoes to keep me from getting my feet wet on this day!"

Within an hour, the two ladies had made it through the first sack and were onto the second. David was kept busy running the peels out to the compost pile in the chicken yard. Mercy only had two of her fingers wrapped due to cuts and, seeing how she had ten fingers in total, that was only twenty percent, which she felt was more than allowable. Abigail had somehow navigated the first sack without a scratch, but Mercy reasoned that was due to her years of experience.

Mercy's hand was blistered and cramping by the time they finished with the last potatoes. Her back and forearms ached, but she had won. There were a good two hours before the supper rush. Mercy stretched her sore back and wiped her sweaty brow, then she pulled off her apron and hung it in its place.

"A deal's a deal," said Abigail. "Go have fun."

Outside, Mercy found Abe and Benjamin running hoes through the garden. "Let's go, boys. Abigail said to be back in an hour!"

While the boys put their tools away, Mercy described in detail the mountain she had overcome to provide them all with this opportunity. Showing them her bandaged fingers and blisters, she said, "I had to pry the knife from my hand when we were finished."

"How's it feel to do real work for a change?" teased Benjamin.

"Yeah, our hands are worse off than yours," agreed Abe, holding up his own calloused hands.

"It was a mountain, and you boys ought to be grateful! Why, if I hadn't peeled nearly two hundred of 'em, you'd still be workin' that garden!" Mercy said with a scowl.

"Alright, Mercy, we're just teasing is all. Let's go for a swim and cool down. Your face looks flushed," Benjamin said with a smirk.

At the pond, the boys stripped down to their trousers and dove in while Mercy sat out on a tree trunk that had fallen into the water. As she lay back with her feet dangling in the cool water, she dreamed of home, of Papa, of her mother before she died. Would she ever know a life like that again? She closed her eyes and tried to dream of what it would be like if the war ended, she grew up, met a handsome man like her papa, and had a family. She dreamed of holidays and birthdays, of joyful gatherings and peace.

"Mercy. Mercy! Wake up, it's time to be heading back."

Someone shook her gently and Mercy opened her eyes. The sun had begun its descent to the west, though it had done little to relieve the heat. It took her a moment to place herself.

"Mercy, it's time we were back," repeated David.

Lifting her head to sit up, she found herself nose to nose with a giant bullfrog. Mercy let out a shriek and writhed to get clear of the colossal frog. She lost her balance and slid off the log, into the pond. Regaining her footing, Mercy blasted out of the water in a sputtering fury. David stood facing her on the other side of the log, a look of terror on his face. Benjamin and Abe waded over to survey the scene and, upon seeing Mercy soaking wet and covered with debris, Abe burst out laughing.

"Goodness, Mercy, if you're gonna go swimmin', you have to at least take your dress off."

"David Young, you'll pay for this!" Mercy fumed.

"I didn't know you'd fall off the log, Mercy. Honest, I was just havin' a little fun," David replied.

"What happened?" asked Benjamin, attempting to be sympathetic.

"That little rat put a frog on my chest while I was sleeping," Mercy said through clenched teeth.

"He what?" Abe exclaimed, bursting out in a fresh round of laughter.

"I really am sorry, Mercy. I won't ever do it again as long as I live. I swear," pleaded David.

Trudging to shore, Mercy began wringing out her dress. She fought back tears as her emotions flickered from rage to grief and back again. This time, her brother's savagery had gone too far. She was used to their foolery, and usually turned a blind eye as they took turns pranking one another. Mercy, for the most part, had been exempt from the foolishness, and for that reason, she had tolerated it with little complaint. But this? This had wounded her pride.

"Mercy, we do need to be headin' back now," Benjamin said.

"Look on the bright side, you got to cool down," said Abe.

"I didn't know a frog could cause so much trouble," lamented David.

"You're blaming the frog?!"

With that, Mercy hiked up her dress and marched towards the tavern with the little boys almost jogging to keep up.

At the tavern, Abigail met them at the back door. "You're late," she said, then gasped at the state of Mercy's dress. "Lord have mercy, child. Did you go swimming in your dress?"

Striding forward, Mercy fell into Abigail's arms, sobbing.

Abigail gave Benjamin a confused look.

"David sort of startled her, and she fell off the log, ma'am," Benjamin explained.

Abigail's expression softened, and she led Mercy into the house. David followed close behind, confessing his regret every step of the way.

"I'm afraid we don't have time to clean you up proper. You'll have to dry off as best you can and put on a fresh dress. Once we're finished tonight, I'm sure David here wouldn't mind drawing you a hot bath to help wash away the results of his foolery," Abigail said, eyeing David.

"No, ma'am, I wouldn't mind," David quickly agreed with a big gulp.

"Good. Now, it's fixin' to get busy, so get cleaned up quick as you can."

Abigail was right. The general's arrival and subsequent training regimen had left the militiamen with a powerful hunger. Even with all those peeled potatoes from earlier, the tavern still ran out. That night an exciting guest showed up at the tavern and requested to see Mercy. Henry asked the man if he'd be able to stay for an hour until closing time, and have dinner with them.

When the last of the customers had left, Henry led the man back to the kitchen where Mercy was preparing some biscuits for their supper.

"Miss Mercy?" a soft voice interrupted her.

Turning around, Mercy nearly fell over. There, right in front of her, stood Mr. Isaac Hadley. She hadn't seen him since the wagon trip back to Cambridge. He stood there holding a black brimmed hat in his hand. He was trembling a little, his eyes glistened with tears, and his look was soft and kind.

"Miss Mercy, I—I never got the chance to thank you for saving my life," he said, fumbling with his hat. "I've been a nobody most all my life. Never done nothin' worth someone taking notice. I wanted you to know I've spent the better part of a month laying on a cot with nothin' to do 'cept ponder on why you'd do that for me." He wiped away a tear that had shaken loose and looked at the floor. "I can't for the life of me figure out why."

The old man stood looking so broken and lost there was nothing for it. Mercy brushed the flour off her hands and crossed the short distance between them, throwing her arms around him.

"I'm glad you're here," Mercy said.

Mr. Hadley steadied himself with his cane and threw his free arm around her as tears traced their way down his face.

"We'd be honored if you'd join us for dinner," Henry said. "We've already got your place set."

Mr. Hadley nodded that he would.

That night, they ate and laughed and shared stories. Mr. Hadley had a wonderful laugh and a friendly spirit; he instantly took a liking to David. He even told a story of how he had pranked his own older sister with a frog. Mercy sat back and pondered her growing family. She felt satisfied, full of joy and light. It was as though Mr. Hadley had always belonged there. Perhaps he had been waiting all this time, waiting for someone to rescue him.

Chapter 9

Mercy groaned as the drums of the Continental army drove her from sleep. The entire bed began to squirm as the boys came to their senses.

"Why do they keep doing that?" whined David.

"It's the general," groaned Benjamin.

"Even on Sunday?" Mercy pouted.

It was the third day in a row the drums had woken up the town at dawn. General Washington was determined to make an army out of the militia, and the townsfolk were being transformed by default.

"Maybe we can go back to sleep when they're finished," moaned Abe.

But this was not to be. No sooner had the drums ceased than Abigail called up the stairs for breakfast. The Youngs piled out of bed, got dressed, and staggered their way downstairs.

Abigail was already in her apron, humming hymns as she set the table. She was always so bubbly in the morning, it disgusted Mercy. How could anyone be that excited to be roused from their dreams, flushed from their bed, and forced out into the cruel and unforgiving world of reality?

"Now, there's a dreary sight," she said as they reached the bottom of the stairs. "It's a beautiful morning this mornin', the birds are singin' the Lord's praises, and here you all are, looking as if someone walked over your grave."

"Mrs. Abigail, how on earth do you know what the birds are singin' about?" grumbled David, sliding into his chair.

Benjamin clapped his hand over David's mouth. "Sorry, ma'am, he can be a might testy in the mornin'."

"That makes two of us," said Abe.

Abigail burst out laughing. "Why, it seems the good general has gone and got under your skin, boys."

"Humph," added Mercy, which brought out a new round of laughter.

Just then, Henry walked in. "Sounds like we'll be having church on the green this morning. General Washington is requiring the entire army, except for the sentries, to attend. They're moving the benches out as seating for the ladies and small children, but the men will all have to stand."

"Won't that be a sight to see," said Abigail, beaming.

"Stand?!" wailed David, dropping his forehead to the table.

As Abigail had predicted, the green was a sight to see. Companies of soldiers formed a blocky arch facing the pulpit with the townsfolk at the center. Mercy and Abigail took their seats in the pews while the boys and Henry stood in the back.

When it came time to sing the old hymns, the chorus was breathtaking. With so many voices lifted up, she was sure God could hear them. She wondered if Papa could hear them too. Then came the preaching. Reverend Greene spoke from the book of John about freedom, he spoke about setting captives free, and about fighting the good fight. The service went on for nearly two hours. Mercy didn't dare look back at the boys, whom she was sure were suffering from awful stiff legs by this time. David could scarcely stand still for two minutes on his own without the promise of a proper reward. For their sakes, and the sake of her aching backside, she hoped that the reverend would close soon.

At last, it was time to sing the final hymn. Mercy wasn't sure if it was relief or that the reverend had done his job well, but the men really belted out the final refrain in grand fashion. The assembly was released with a prayer, and the soldiers marched back to camp.

The boys limped over to where Abigail and Mercy were carrying on a conversation with a few of the other ladies from town. Henry carried David on his shoulders, struggling to hide his own stiff limp.

"Oh, the men are here," Abigail said. She conducted a small curtsy, and smiling politely, turned from her conversation. "Wasn't that service just divine?"

"Yes, a timely message," replied Henry.

"I can't feel my legs," Abe said, perplexed.

"Oh, you poor dears," Abigail said, pinching his cheek. "I know just the thing to fix you right up. Let's have a picnic down by the pond today. That'll give you boys a chance to relax and limber up a bit."

Mercy and Abigail gathered a basket and some sandwiches while the boys gathered the fishing canes and a few worms. Henry grabbed a blanket and a pail of water with a dipper. The sun had come out and the temperature had risen several degrees. Mercy took the blanket from Henry and spread it under an old cottonwood tree near the log she had so rudely been roused from only a few days ago.

The boys set out their rods before coming for a sandwich. Henry didn't even make it to lunch. He leaned back against the mighty trunk and pulled his brim hat down over his eyes, and that was that. The boys, being the savages they were, wolfed down their sandwiches and were already stripping for a swim. Abigail shrieked and laughed as the boys plowed into the pond, sending a spray of water in every direction.

"Now that we're alone, I wanted to tell you something, Mercy," Abigail said. "Henry has a few contacts in Boston, friends, who used to supply the tavern. He asked if they would be willing to check with the magistrate and see if your father's name was on the prisoner registry."

Mercy sat up, her chest tightening.

Abigail took her hand. "You children were right, your father is here, in the harbor. Unfortunately, the redcoats are still rather sore about the battle that day. They will not be releasing any of the insurrectionists under any circumstances by order of King George. To tell the truth of it, it sounds like your father was lucky he had skills that make him of use on the ship. Most of the other prisoners were tried and executed."

Mercy held her chest. "Papa." She looked out over the pond, watching the boys wrestle about, laughing and splashing wildly. "Does Benjamin know?"

"Henry's gonna give him the details today."

"Papa didn't want war, he just wanted us to be free. Is that such a terrible crime?" asked Mercy.

"No, child, that's not a crime at all. Your papa loved you enough to lay down his life if necessary, to see his babies live free. There's no crime in that at all."

"Will we ever get him back?" asked Mercy.

"Only the Lord knows the answer to that question, but he'd want us to believe and hope," Abigail said.

Mercy laid back on the blanket and closed her eyes. She was grateful that Papa was alive, but to have him so close in the harbor was more of a cruel joke than a comfort. So long as he was alive, there was hope of getting him back, and she determined to never let go of that hope. She tried to imagine him on that awful ship, but it was too much, and she decided it was better to remember him at home. She knew Papa would be worried about them and she wished there was a way they could reach him to let him know they were alright and being looked after. It looked like Papa was going to have to believe and hope, too.

"Abigail?"

"Yes, child."

"Thank you."

"For what?"

"For giving us a home."

Abigail squeezed her hand. "Thank you for giving us a family, even if it's just for a little while," she whispered.

After a moment or two, Mercy sat up. "I think I'll try some fishin'," she said, picking up one of the canes. She decided to set it out near the large log since the boys were making a mess of everything else. A gentle breeze made the stalks of grass dance at the edge of the pond, and a red dragonfly glided gently onto the end of her rod. Mercy watched the little creature clean its face as it sunned itself.

All at once, Mercy's rod jumped from the forked stick and shot towards the water. Mercy pounced on it at the water's edge and set the hook. The rod bent violently, and the line shot off to the left. Mercy struggled to hang on. Feeling like the rod would break if she didn't do something, she waded into the water, refusing to let go.

"Oh, my Lord, Henry! Do something!" Abigail yelled.

Henry leapt to his feet and charged into the water after Mercy. "Hang on, Mercy!" he yelled.

As Henry approached, the fish made a wild run to the right. Mercy swung the rod violently to keep up, catching Henry with the hilt square in the chest and knocking him into the water. The boys heard the commotion and joined the fray, shouting advice as Mercy waded deeper and deeper into the pond in a desperate struggle to hold on.

Mercy was nearly waist-deep in the water now, hanging on for dear life as the fish had its way with the rod in her hands. By this time, many of the townsfolk nearby had stopped to watch the action. Henry wrapped his arms around Mercy to keep her on her feet. He was covered with mud and sticks and laughed wildly as he cheered her on.

At last, the beast grew weary, and Henry made his move. He dove under the water, following Mercy's line. Everyone held their breath. The water began to churn violently as he reached the end of it, and Mercy clung to the rod, white-knuckled, waiting for him to come up. Henry broke the surface of the water sputtering and slowly raised himself. In his arms he carried the biggest catfish any of them had ever seen. It was twenty pounds if it was an ounce.

Around the pond, everyone cheered the soggy heroes. Mercy and Henry made their way to the shore, where he gave a bow, and Mercy, following his lead, gave a curtsy. Abigail was waiting for them when they reached the shore.

"Well, that was a show, make no mistake," she laughed. "Oh, just look at you two . . . and in your Sunday dress."

Mercy had forgotten about her dress. "Ugh, I'm sorry, Abigail . . . I just couldn't let it get away."

"It's no skin off my nose." She shrugged with a grin. "This week you're all doin' your own laundry." She poked her finger in Henry's chest with a sly smile. "All of you." And she walked back to the blanket and sat down.

That night, after the laundry was finished and drying on the line, they ate a feast of catfish with potatoes. Mercy had requested Mr. Hadley join them and later, after they had all eaten their fill, they sat back around a small campfire, Henry smoking his pipe, as Mr. Hadley shared tales of his battles during the French and Indian War. At last, the drums sounded, and Mr. Hadley had to scurry back to camp. It had been a full day, a good day, and Mercy went to bed grateful for having lived it.

Chapter 10

October 16, 1775

It has become apparent that the only way to get Papa back is to win the war. The nearly constant skirmishes between the Continentals and the redcoats have eroded any hope of a peaceful resolution. My hope has been enriched by the ever-increasing military professionalism of the Continentals.

It seems that the good general is making headway with his army, they march right smartly around the green now. The manner of the men has changed as well and they conduct themselves with a greater sense of decorum, even in the tavern. The camps have even been brought to order; a feat that seemed impossible a mere three months ago. The spirit of the army is high, though it has done little to help them drive the redcoats from Boston.

Today was my birthday, and while it has only been a year since my last, I have all but forgotten that life. This war is all-consuming, and impossible to escape. From the time we wake up in the morning, it's drums and marching, cannon and musket fire, more drums, and soldiers everywhere.

Benjamin gave me some ribbons for my hair, and the boys brought me flowers. Poor Abe couldn't resist adding a couple thistle blossoms to the bouquet and nearly cried as Abigail removed the stickers. Henry brought back a new dress from New York, and Abigail baked me a cake with real icing. It was a beautiful day, and I have much to be thankful for.

The leaves on the trees have transformed into brilliant yellows, reds, and oranges. When the wind blows, they fall to the ground like colorful snowflakes. The mornings begin with a chill, but by noon it's quite comfortable. Henry is going to take Abe and Benjamin on a deer hunt Sunday afternoon, and Benjamin is nearly raw with excitement, though he tries to hide it. Mr. Hadley said that he'll teach us how to snare rabbits soon so that we'll have some for stews. If I'm being honest, I'd take a rabbit stew over most meals, especially the way Abigail makes it.

The drums have just sounded, and the camps will be going dark soon. My mind seems to be under the general's command as it responds to his infernal drums as though I were one of his soldiers. It's time I was off to bed.

Mercy Young, 13 years old.

The day started off with a bang, literally. Cannons erupted from the harbor, sending clods of dirt and debris high into the air below the town. The Continental cannons answered with their own volley, sending bits of Boston equally high. The exchange lasted only a few moments and then all was quiet again.

"What was that all about?" asked David.

"They don't want us to forget they're there, do they?" replied Henry.

"How could we?" retorted Abigail. "They've got us livin' on all manner of crudeness and wild game, thanks to their blockade. Why, a blind man could see that it'd be better for both sides if they'd just sail away and leave us alone."

"They've too much pride for that," said Henry. "I don't think we've even begun to taste the king's wrath. Those poor devils in Boston are only buying time. Soon a proper army will arrive, and the war will really begin."

Everyone in the room sat in stunned silence. Henry looked up from the paper he was reading.

"You mean this isn't even a war yet?" asked Abe.

"I'm afraid not," said Henry. "This was just the first spark. Eventually, the whole British army will arrive, and that's why the general's working so hard to turn the militias into an army. If he's not ready before they arrive, those boys will be crushed in short order."

"When will the army arrive?" asked Mercy.

"No one knows. They haven't arrived yet, which means George has underestimated Congress's resolve thus far, but it can't drag on like this forever." Henry cleared his throat. "But we can't do anything about that today, and we've got plenty of work to do, so we'd better get about it."

The family huddle broke and each of them got busy with their morning chores. Mercy began working some batter for biscuits while pondering Henry's words.

Later that afternoon, the four Youngs went on a foraging mission collecting chestnuts to roast. The trees were plentiful and easy enough to find. They worked their way down a hillside and along a narrow creek. Mercy's apron was two-thirds full and getting quite heavy as they walked. They had just rounded a bend when Benjamin halted and motioned for them to duck behind a ledge. He peaked his head out and then back again, breathing heavily.

"What is it?" asked Mercy.

"Redcoats." Benjamin held his finger to his lips. "Don't make a sound." He peered around the corner of the ledge for a better look.

"What are they doing?" whispered Mercy.

"Same thing we are, it looks like. Collecting nuts."

"What are we gonna do?" asked Abe.

"I think they're fixin' to come this way," said Benjamin. "I don't think they want to be found any more than we do. They're a long way from Boston." He paused to think for a moment. "We'll head up the creek edge 'til we make it around the next bend. Then we'll head up the hill and get back to the tavern. Mercy, you're gonna have to leave the nuts here. You won't be able to run up the hill without spilling some and makin' noise. Dump 'em out real quiet. "

Mercy nodded her head and lowered one corner of her apron. The chestnuts spilled out with minimal clatter.

"Let's go," said Benjamin, and they set off down the creek.

The going was slow at first, on account of the noisy leaves, but once they rounded the corner of the creek, they quickened the pace up the hill and jogged the quarter mile back to the tavern.

Henry was just returning from the smokehouse with a side of bacon when they trotted into the yard. "What's the hurry?" he asked as Benjamin pulled up huffing.

"Redcoats!" Benjamin replied. "In the ravine."

"Where?!"

Benjamin pointed in the direction they had just come. "Down by the creek," he said, still panting.

Henry ran into the tavern and appeared a moment later with a young Continental officer. "Tell him what you just told me!"

"There are redcoats down the ravine by the creek," Benjamin said, pointing again.

"How many?" asked the officer.

"Four or five, I think. We didn't stay long," replied Benjamin.

The officer nodded his thanks and sprinted off towards the army camps.

"You did the right thing," said Henry. "You all best get inside and get yourselves some water. Don't come out until I give the word."

As the four Youngs filed through the back door, they ran into Abigail in the kitchen. She looked them over, all red-faced and Mercy's hair filled with twigs and leaves. "Good heavens, children, what have you gone and done now?!"

"There were redcoats!" David answered excitedly.

Just then, twenty soldiers tromped by the window, led by the young officer. They stopped for a moment to talk to Henry and then marched off at the double quick. The soldiers fanned out at the crest of the hill and proceeded down the ravine and out of sight.

"What on earth are they doin' so far out of Boston?" Abigail asked no one in particular.

"They were collecting nuts, as far as I could tell," said Benjamin.

"We had to leave all of ours. Mercy had nearly a full apron." Abe frowned.

"You brought back the most important thing, and that's all that matters," Abigail said, giving him a half-hug. "Now, why don't you all get washed up and get a quick bite before things get busy."

Mercy went upstairs to change her dress and apron, and on her way back down, she heard Abe call out, "They're coming back!"

Mercy raced back up the stairs and opened the window. Sure enough, at the top of the ravine, Mercy could just make out two columns of Continental soldiers with a small column of red in between. As they drew closer, Mercy counted four redcoats being marched at bayonet point. Reaching the tavern, the officer nodded to Henry and continued marching right under Mercy's window. The redcoats looked nervous and tired; their uniforms were far from the condition of those who had taken the green in Lexington. They drug their feet as the Continentals prodded them along.

Mercy wanted to hate them, to see them as monsters who only devoured and destroyed, but she couldn't. Seeing them so pitiful and afraid, they were just men, just people, lost and far from home. As they marched on towards the army camp, Mercy knew there would be many men like them, like Mr. Hadley, like her father, who would be captured or killed before the war ended. *Is freedom worth it?*

At supper, Benjamin shared what he had overheard a couple officers say about the redcoats they captured. The redcoats had been interrogated and disclosed they were short on rations due to a maggot infestation on one of the ships sent from England. The soldiers in Boston were beginning to suffer breakdowns over being stuck in one place for so long. The British general was at his wits' end as parliament wanted him to deal with the rebels but sent him no additional troops to rout them. They were ill-prepared for winter, but well supplied for war, as the king made sure to send plenty of munitions. Unfortunately, it sounded like the only thing stopping the Continental army from crushing them was that they lacked the powder and cannons to do so.

That night, as she lay in bed, Mercy wondered about freedom, about what it meant to be free, what it meant to be a slave. A slave doesn't have control over their own life, to live how they believe they should live. Was it possible to really live a life that wasn't free? If it weren't, then living as a slave was barely better than being dead, except if one were alive, they have the hope of one day being free. If one were living already as good as dead, then perhaps dying for the chance to be free wasn't that far of a stretch. And in this war, which was the greater stretch—a man willing to die to be free, or a man willing to die to keep others from being free?

Chapter 11

Sunday finally arrived and, as promised, Mr. Hadley met the Youngs at the tavern for their first trapping lesson. Mercy met him in the yard with a hug while the boys tripped over one another in their excited anticipation. In one hand, he carried a small coil of wire, and in the other, his cane. Mr. Hadley smiled broadly at their excitement, and with a twinkle in his eye, he promised them quite the adventure.

The five of them set off into the woods, west of Cambridge, the leaves crunching loudly under their feet. After about a hundred yards or so, Mr. Hadley halted and gestured with his cane at a small, rounded opening in a patch of briers. He knelt down on his good knee and pointed to a small mound of dark pellets. The Youngs leaned in for a closer look.

"This is a good spot. There are plenty of droppings, and I'll bet there's a rabbit hole in them briers." He pointed again at the rounded opening. "There's a bit of fur here on these stickers, which means it's a good tight spot, he'll have trouble finding a way 'round our noose."

Mr. Hadley stretched out a length of the thin wire about as long as his arm and cut it off with a pair of pliers. He pointed out a sapling branch, about as big a round as his thumb, a couple of feet from the hole. At one end of the wire, he made a noose, and on the other end he attached to the sapling roughly four feet off the ground. About six inches up the wire from the noose, he added a short hardwood stick. The Youngs watched in wonder as he worked.

At last, Mr. Hadley bent the sapling down and held it there with the small stick by wedging it between the ground and a briar stalk near the opening of the hole. Lastly, he molded the wire into a perfect circle that filled the entire opening with the bottom of the loop resting about two inches off the ground.

"When the hare hops out of this hole tonight, he'll get caught in the noose, pull this twig free, and the sapling will spring upright. Mark my words, we'll have a rabbit hangin' here in the mornin'," he said with a satisfied smile.

"That's brilliant!" said Benjamin.

"My father was a trapper," Mr. Hadley said. "He didn't know much about fatherin', but he did know the woods."

They continued a little way further and Mr. Hadley stopped again. He waited a few moments while glancing around and then looked at the Youngs. Finally, he asked, "Do you see it?"

"See what?" asked David.

"The rabbit tunnel."

Mercy began searching desperately; she was fiercely competitive and wanted to impress Mr. Hadley. She only had a moment before Abe pointed to a patch of brown, dried grasses.

"Is that it?" he asked.

Mercy followed his finger and sure enough, near a place where an old log lay, was another perfect circle with room only for a rabbit.

"That's it!" declared Mr. Hadley. He ruffled Abe's shaggy hair in satisfaction.

This time, he cut off the length of wire and handed it to Benjamin. "Show me what you know, son," he said with a confident smile.

Benjamin made a crude noose on one end. Mercy picked him out a good sapling nearby, and Abe brought him a hardwood stick. Benjamin attached the wire to the sapling and then put Abe's stick in place. He bent the sapling over and wedged the stick between the ground and the old log, just like Mr. Hadley had done. Next, he began working on his noose, shaping it to the hole as he had seen. All of a sudden, his arm was jerked upwards, and he found himself snared in his own trap.

Mr. Hadley let out a hearty laugh, slapping his knee. "If I had a nickel for every time I caught myself, I'd be a rich man!" They all laughed, including Benjamin.

Mr. Hadley helped Benjamin reset his snare, and when it was all finished, it was near-invisible. As they continued on that afternoon, Mr. Hadley taught the Youngs to read game trails, identify animal tracks, and where to look for sign. He always had the children find the rabbit trails, and they took turns setting the snares. Abe had the same misfortune as Benjamin and ended up tangled in this own snare.

When it came down to Mercy's turn, she was terribly nervous. She found the perfect rabbit tunnel leading into a pile of fallen branches. There was plenty of sign nearby, and it was fresh. The only sapling available was a mite stout, and she had to lift her weight up on it to bend it all the way over. Due to the extra strength of the tree, she had a terrible time finding a suitable anchor. At last, with a little help from Mr. Hadley, she was able to secure the wire. She gently spread the noose, careful not to put any tension on the anchor, and when she stepped back, it looked as good as any of them.

"Why, we'll make a woodsman out of you yet!" said Mr. Hadley.

Mercy beamed, though she tried to hide it.

They set several more snares that afternoon before returning to the tavern. Henry asked Mr. Hadley to stay for dinner, and together they shared the tales of the day's adventures. Mercy teased the boys about getting caught in their own traps, the boys teased Mercy about not being able to secure her own snare, but it was all in good fun. Mercy had no idea that saving Mr. Hadley would add so much joy to her family and so much warmth to her world.

At last, the drums called Mr. Hadley back to camp. "Don't forget to check those first thing tomorrow. If you wait too long, that ol' sly coywolf is gonna steal your dinner," he said, and bid them all a good night.

That night, the Youngs' bed squirmed with anxious young trappers. The worst of all was David.

"Benjamin, do you think we'll catch a rabbit or two tonight? Or do you think it'll be more like six or seven?"

"I dunno, buddy. I've never trapped anything before, but Mr. Hadley seemed pretty confident," answered Benjamin.

"Do you think a coywolf will get 'em?"

"It's possible, they're pretty good at finding an easy meal."

"Do you suppose we're catching some right now?"

"Go to bed, David. We'll find out in the morning."

The bed was quiet for a moment or two.

"Benjamin?"

"What?"

"Are you excited?"

"Yes, now go to bed."

"Good, I'm exci—"

"David Jerimiah Young, if you say one more word before that blasted drummer beats that drum in the mornin', you will regret it!" Mercy growled.

Immediately, the bed went still.

When morning came, the Youngs blasted out of bed. Throwing on their clothes, they raced down the stairs, bumping into a shocked Abigail who was just donning her apron.

"My goodness, what's all this?" she asked.

"Mr. Hadley said we have to check the snares first thing," replied David.

"Not before you finish your chores and get some breakfast," Abigail said.

"But the coywolves . . ." lamented Abe.

"Not before breakfast! Now, go on and get started and Mercy and I will have something for you as soon as you're done."

The Youngs sprang into action, the thought of a coywolf stealing their hard-earned rabbits driving them on.

Outside, David raced past Henry, who was harnessing the team for a supply run, with a basket full of eggs. Next was Abe, carrying two buckets of water from the well that sloshed as he trotted to the kitchen door. Chunks of wood exploded in all directions as Benjamin laid waste to his morning quota. Again, Abe and David ran past, brandishing a pitchfork, shovel, and wheelbarrow.

Mercy caught a glimpse of Henry watching with amusement as the hay flew from the horse stall.

Abigail called for breakfast, and everyone came running. Abe and David, looking a frightful mess, made their way towards the table but were cut off by Abigail, who redirected them to the washbasin. Benjamin had bits of bark and splinters in his hair and the wisdom to follow the boys to the wash. Even Mercy had been less-than-careful while making breakfast and her apron bore several stains.

When they finally sat for breakfast, Henry thanked them all for their hard work that morning and said grace. The table erupted in a fury of eating as the Youngs inhaled their food. As soon as they finished, they begged their leave.

"May we go now, ma'am?" David asked.

"Alright, but hurry back. We've a full day ahead of us," Abigail said.

"I'll only wait a short while Mercy, if you're not back, I'll have to leave without you," Henry said.

Nodding, Mercy raced out the door to catch the boys, who were already running for the trees.

It was a beautiful morning in the woods. The air was crisp and fresh, and sunlight made the golden leaves on the forest floor glow with beautiful radiance. Mercy held her breath as they approached the first snare in the briar patch.

"We got one!" shouted Abe, running up to the sapling.

Sure enough, hanging from the wire a couple feet off the ground was a good-sized cottontail. Benjamin carefully spread the loop and pulled it off its neck and handed the rabbit to David.

"You can carry the first one."

David beamed. "How many more do you think there are?"

"Won't know 'til we check 'em," Benjamin replied.

After resetting the snare, they were off to the next one. At the second snare, the rabbit had pushed the wire out of the way and brushed past it. Benjamin fixed the wire and added a bit of grass for better camouflage, and they were off to the next one. The next snare was Abe's, and like the first, a rabbit hung neatly from the sapling.

"I got one!" Abe said, holding his prize in the air.

Benjamin helped him reset the snare and the four of them moved on to the next one with growing anticipation. At Mercy's snare, they were met with a tragic sight. The head of a rabbit hung from the sapling; fur littered the forest floor. Mercy felt devastated. She had done well, her snare had worked, and yet, there was no prize, only the disappointment of being cheated.

"It looks like Mr. Hadley was right about the coywolf..." said David sorrowfully.

"I don't think it's any use resetting this one," said Benjamin. "Let's check the rest and get back."

"Maybe Mr. Hadley can teach us how to catch a coywolf," said Abe.

Benjamin put his arm around Mercy's shoulder. "I'm sure he could help you catch this bandit."

By the time they finished checking the snares, they had four rabbits, and had found a second loss to the coywolf. Mercy felt both satisfied and disappointed, but more than that, she felt a new connection to the woods. They had become a part of the struggle of life and death; they had both outwitted and been outwitted, and she wanted more of it.

Abigail cheered the trapper heroes as they returned with their catch.

"These will make a splendid stew. Mr. Hadley will be thrilled to hear about your success!" Abigail said.

"We lost two to the coywolf," David said indignantly.

"Mercy, if you're coming with me, we have to go now," interrupted Henry patiently.

As they rode along, Mercy told Henry about the coywolf, about feeling disappointed and satisfied, about feeling connected to the woods. Henry just listened to her as she talked.

"You are an amazing girl, Mercy. I don't know how Abigail and I have lasted this long without you, without all of you," he said. "Even in the midst of this terrible war where brothers have risen against one another, and times are more difficult than anyone can remember, I find myself smiling more than I ever did before because the four of you are here."

Mercy leaned over and rested her head on his arm as they rode.

Chapter 12

November 3, 1775

The wet cool weather we have been experiencing as of late has ushered in a sickness amongst the soldiers in the camps. Dr. Morris has been overrun with new cases of the fever, and more than a few soldiers have already died. Mrs. Abigail and I have been called away on multiple occasions lately to lend a hand. I mostly fetch water and other things the doctor and Mrs. Abigail need. I've never seen so many folks looking so miserable in my life.

Reverend Greene has been forced to conduct his services in the tavern on account of the church being requisitioned as a secondary hospital. Henry heard from his contacts in Boston that the British are faring no better. More boys on both sides have been killed by the fever than each other lately. I pray to the Lord by the hour that this awful cold rain would cease. There has been little joy to be found anywhere as of late. Henry even had to make the supply run to New York without me this time.

I fear for Papa. I don't expect a prison ship is very warm, or that the care of prisoners is anywhere near the care of soldiers. If he passed, it's likely he'd just be dumped in the harbor without anyone to know or care. I wish that dreadful day in Lexington would have never come, but the Lord has seen fit to work it together for good by blessing us with good folks like Henry, Abigail, and Mr. Hadley. It's a kindness I could never repay.

Mercy Young, 13 years old.

Mercy woke to Abigail's gentle shaking. "Don't wake the boys," she whispered. "The doctor came callin' a few moments ago and was near to dropping from exhaustion. He needs a few hours' rest or we'll lose him too."

Mercy got out of bed and crept from the room before getting dressed. She placed a handkerchief over her nose and mouth and put on a clean apron. Abigail met her at the bottom of the stairs and handed her a couple of bread rolls from the night before.

"I'm afraid this is going to have to pass as breakfast," she said.

Mercy and Abigail made their way to the chapel as the grey hue of predawn shone in the eastern sky. The rain was little more than a mist, but coupled with the breeze, it drove the cold into the bones. The chapel was filled with the dim glow of lanterns, the pews were filled with feverish patients, and the smell of vomit nearly overpowered the senses. For the first several days of helping the doctor, Mercy had to keep forcing down her own reflexes that repulsed at the smell, but now she had grown so accustomed that it had little effect.

Picking up a bucket of water and a dipper, Mercy began working up and down the rows of pews, offering water to those who could keep it down. Here and there, nurses gave medicines, swapped cooling rags, and cleaned up vomit. Abigail joined them in their care.

Approaching a pew, Mercy noticed its occupant looked curiously out of place. The man seemed neither in distress nor well. His color, even in the dim light, was pale, but his forehead bore no sweat. In fact, other than his color, the man looked quite peaceful. Abigail noticed her pause and joined her at his bench, then she turned to Mercy.

"You can move along, Mercy, he won't be needing any more water now," she said softly.

Looking back at the man, she understood. He was dead. A swarm of emotions swept over her, and she set her bucket down. He had died alone, no family, no friends, no one by his side, and with no more care than a "move along." Mercy didn't know why, but she took his cold hand in hers and said, "Goodbye sir, I'm sorry you're gone." Then she let his lifeless grip slip from hers.

Turning to Abigail, she said, "It isn't fair." Then, collapsing into Abigail's apron, she sobbed.

Abigail allowed her a good cry before gently reminding her of the living who still needed her tender care. "We're all they have now, Mercy, and we must be strong."

Picking up her bucket, Mercy took a last glance at the poor stranger and moved along. It was awful enough to have men dying on the battlefield, but this was a whole other level of injustice. She did her best to be friendly and smile as she offered each patient water. Some were too ill to respond, while others readily lapped up the water, only to vomit it right back out. Some of them just wanted her to stay by their side, their fevers causing them to become delirious and mistake her for loved ones. It broke her heart to have to move on as they pleaded with her to stay.

At dawn, the drummer caused the patients to stir, and after a short while, the general arrived and spoke with the nurses. His face looked grim as he surveyed the scene. At his command, a couple of soldiers entered the chapel and carried out the man who had died. Shortly after he left, Dr. Morris returned, looking a little rested, and began going over the patients one by one.

Around noon, the situation went from bad to worse. The doctor informed Abigail and the nurses that he was nearly out of fever medicine, and they would have to triage the patients—only giving it to those most likely to survive. Mercy was busy boiling rags when she heard the news and, pausing for a moment, she pleaded with the Lord to provide aid in some way. Things seemed so desperate; it would surely take a miracle.

Suddenly, Abe came running up to the chapel. Abigail saw him through the window and met him at the door.

"What is it, child?"

"Dave . . ." he said, gasping. "David's got the fever!"

"What?!" cried Abigail, turning pale.

"All of a sudden, he just started throwin' up. Henry carried him to bed, but he's hot as fire and we don't know what to do."

The doctor came over just in time to hear the news. His face looked grave, but he managed a smile and told Abigail and Mercy to go. Together they ran for the tavern. Abigail didn't slow down when they arrived, but ran right up the stairs and chased the boys out.

"You must all stay out; we can't have the fever spreading." She said it kindly, but with enough edge to be understood.

"Did you bring medicine?" asked Henry.

Abigail asked the boys to go downstairs to the kitchen and fix Mercy and her some lunch. As soon as the boys were gone, she turned to Henry.

"There isn't any," she said, fighting back tears.

"I don't understand."

"We've used it all, Henry. There isn't anything left to give him." Her lips quivered, and she gripped the front of her dress in desperation.

Henry looked at Mercy, who was already in tears. "There has to be something . . ."

Abigail clung to his hand and took a deep breath. "Mercy and I are going to need a constant supply of cool rags—the colder, the better. And we're gonna' need 'em boiled after they've been used."

Henry nodded and set off down the stairs to collect supplies and get the water boiling.

"Mercy, I need you to get some chicken broth warming. Teach the boys the system we used at the chapel, and bring the broth when it's ready," Abigail said.

As Mercy turned towards the stairs, Abigail called after her, "He's gonna be alright, Mercy, we're here now."

Mercy did what she was told. Tearing some cloth into strips, she showed the boys how to make the cooling rags. Henry brought in fresh cool water from the well. One bucket he gave to the boys, the other he used for boiling rags. Mercy asked Henry to fetch her a chicken and Henry darted off to the henhouse.

Mercy had just gotten her water to boiling when Henry returned, covered in feathers, with Mercy's chicken. She thanked him with an absent-minded little giggle and put the chicken in the water. As it simmered, she snacked on the lunch the boys had made for her.

"Mercy?" It was Abe. "Is he gonna be okay?"

Putting on the most confident face she could muster, she answered, "He'll be alright."

"But the fever got Mama."

Mercy could see the worry in his eyes. "He's gonna be fine, Abe," was all she could say.

When the broth was finished, Mercy poured it into a bowl and brought it to Abigail. When she looked at David, his eyes were closed, but like the men in the chapel, he was not at peace. He wiggled around uncomfortably, his hair was wet with sweat, but his body shivered. Abigail traded out his cooling rag with a fresh one.

Hours passed as they tried everything they knew to bring his temperature down. Henry had checked again with the doctor about the medicine, but the army had already requisitioned all the medicine around—even New York had nothing left to give. Henry closed the tavern for the day, and the reverend came to pray with them.

A loud knocking around nine o'clock sent Mercy running for the door. As she reached it, Mr. Hadley came bursting in.

"I came as soon as I heard," he said, heading for the kitchen. "Mercy, put some fresh water on to boil."

Mercy obeyed. Everyone stood in stunned confusion, watching him. From a rough satchel, he pulled out several long strips of what appeared to be tree bark.

He pointed a thick finger at Benjamin. "Tomorrow, you and your brothers go to the black willow trees down by the pond and fetch back as much bark as you can carry. Now, watch what I do. You're gonna want to slice it real fine like this," he said as he used his knife to slice the bark into fine strips. "When you get a good amount about like this, add it to the boiling water and let it simmer for several minutes." He added a handful of the bark to the water.

"What are you making?" asked Henry.

"Medicine," he replied. "A Mohawk Indian taught it to my father. It will bring his fever down. It's a kind of tea."

When the medicine had steeped for several minutes, Mr. Hadley poured some into a mug. "Let it cool just a little, and have the lad drink it. You'll see," he said with a confident smile. "It'll bring that fever right down."

When the mug had cooled a little, Mercy brought it to Abigail. Mr. Hadley followed her and explained to Abigail what the tea was. Using a spoon, Abigail painstakingly fed David every last drop. Mr. Hadley regrettably took his leave and said that he would stop by in the morning to check on him. "You can give him a fresh dose every four hours or so," he said, and then bid them all goodnight.

Abigail and Mercy took turns watching David through the night, giving him the medicine as Mr. Hadley had instructed. The morning drums found everyone in David's room. The medicine had driven his fever down during the night and he was sitting up in bed, hungry for something to eat.

"You gave us quite the scare, David," Abigail said. "But I believe you're gonna be alright. It may take a few days for it to pass, but thanks to Mr. Hadley, we can keep your fever down."

After a small breakfast, Abigail put David to bed, and it was time for everyone to get about the day. The boys went to the pond to collect more bark, Mercy and Abigail turned it into tea and brought it to the chapel to give to all the soldiers. Over the next week, the sickness began to subside, and the soldiers were able to head back to camp. The doctor rejoiced the day he pulled out of the chapel, and the good reverend rejoiced to move back in. David was back to his usual self, and they all looked forward to a season of Thanksgiving.

Chapter 13

The day of November 16 brought exciting news. The Cambridge Chronicle declared a Celebration of Harvest Thanksgiving. The tavern was abuzz with preparations. Abigail was able to secure several bushels of corn they kept hidden from the military for this very occasion. Henry bartered for a few pumpkins and a few bushels of apples. The boys gathered all the nuts they could find.

Henry took Benjamin on a deer hunt a few days earlier to a "secret spot" his father used to take him. They were gone nearly the entire morning, and Abigail was beginning to worry when they finally pulled down the road in the wagon. When they arrived, Benjamin wore the biggest grin Mercy could ever remember seeing. Not one, but two beautiful bucks lay in the back of their wagon. One had thick antlers with eight points, and the other had thinner antlers with six points.

Benjamin shared the tale with full dramatization. He pretended to pull out the musket and made the motions of loading the weapon the way Henry had shown him. He told them how they had piled brush in the night near an old log on the edge of an opening near the river. They waited patiently and motionless until the sun began to rise. Then, as the grey of predawn gave way to the morning glow, Henry heard something splashing in the river.

Benjamin explained how his heart drummed in his chest as a beautiful doe pranced out into the opening. Henry had told Benjamin to cock back the hammer. Benjamin made the motion of sliding his musket forward on the log and began to take aim.

Everyone held their breath as he told the story. Then, out of nowhere, the big buck had shown up right behind her. Benjamin slowly swung his musket, and everyone held their breath again. Boom! He pulled the imaginary trigger and waved his arm to push away the imaginary smoke that had filled the air.

While they waited for a short while after the shot to give the animal the chance to expire, Henry had reloaded the musket in case the buck needed another shot. Just as he was sliding the ramrod back into its keeper, the second buck had trotted into the opening with its nose to the ground. It paused just long enough where the first buck had been shot for Henry to take a standing shot at it. The ball struck the deer in the spine and dropped right where it stood.

Benjamin dropped to the ground, mimicking the deer. Then, he went over the story of following the blood trail of his buck and finding it. The awful and yet interesting gutting process. The difficult and exhausting drag. And at last, the triumphant ride home. The entire family applauded him as he finished. Mercy hoped that one day she would have the chance to go hunting, though the idea did not seem to be a popular notion for a woman.

The deer hung up in the tree for a couple of days before Henry skinned them and brought them into the house. The entire family processed the deer together and hung the meat in the smokehouse. The smell from the smoking venison made Mercy's mouth water.

Today, it was Mercy's turn to go on an adventure with Henry. The Harvest Thanksgiving celebration called for a special drink: apple cider. Henry harnessed up the team, and Mercy climbed into the wagon. With a quick flick of the reins, they were on their way to the apple orchard.

"Mr. Henry?"

"Yes, Mercy."

"Do you and Mrs. Abigail celebrate Christmas?"

Henry paused a moment to think. "I'd like to say yes, but now that I think about it, we've been so busy with the tavern all these years, and without any young'uns, I guess we've let it slip by. I mean, we attend all the services, and even sing carols with the townsfolk, but other than that . . ."

"That's sad," Mercy said matter-of-factly. "When Papa was home, we used to take the wagon and cut a tree from the woods together. We all made gifts for one another, and Papa would get us candies from the general store. Papa would hunt up a turkey and we'd make dressing. After supper, he'd read to us the story of Jesus' birth from the Bible, and we'd sing carols together."

"That sounds nice," said Henry thoughtfully. "I think I just decided I'd like to celebrate Christmas this year . . . though it's been so long, I'm not sure if I know how," he added.

Mercy put her hand on his. "Don't worry, Mr. Henry, I'm an expert."

Henry chuckled and gave the reins another quick snap.

As they pulled into the orchard, a portly man in a stocking cap met them in front of a whitewashed barn with a large apple painted on it.

"Hello there, Henry," hollered the man.

Henry jumped down and shook the man's hand. "Hello, Gus, got any cider we could take off your hands?"

"I've got two barrels of the good stuff, and another for the kids."

Mercy found herself captivated by the endless rows of gnarly apple trees. Without their leaves, they looked more like something out of a ghost story than beautiful fruit trees. On one end of the field were old thick-branched trees covered in knots where branches had been pruned off over the years. At the other end of the field were young trees with trunks no bigger than her wrist. There must have been hundreds of them. Walking down a row, Mercy imagined the trees in blossom. Beautiful white flowers covered the now barren branches, their white petals falling like snow all around her. The sweet scent filling the air while an army of bees floated from blossom to blossom.

"Mercy?"

It was Henry, and Mercy's beautiful world faded back to the grey fall day, and the trees became gargoyles again.

"Coming."

When she reached the men, Henry was just finishing his goodbye.

"Mr. Henry, we have to return to this place in the spring. I simply must see these dreary trees in blossom. It would be dreadful if my only memory of this orchard is one of ghoulish trees and grey skies, when I'm sure it is simply divine under better circumstances. I, for one, wouldn't want someone's only opinion of me to be of my worst day just because that's the day they should have been so unfortunate to encounter me."

The two of them just stared at her. "Alright, Mercy, if that's the way you feel, I'm sure Gus would love to have us back in the spring."

"That I would, young Miss. And you're quite right, the orchard is stunning in the spring." He smiled proudly.

Henry helped her into the wagon, and they headed for home.

That afternoon, as Mercy and Henry returned to the tavern, the smell of fresh, warm pies greeted them. Abigail took Henry by the arm and led him into the tavern.

"We've got a surprise for you," she said with a sparkle in her eye.

Walking through the kitchen, Mercy followed them. Entering the tavern, she saw the tables had all been slid together, making one long table down the center of the room. The boys were working feverishly, sweeping the floor, dusting cobwebs, and polishing a couple of candelabras Abigail had dug up.

"We'll put the cider over here," she said, motioning to the bar countertop. "And the food will run down the center of the table. What do you think?" she asked.

"It's amazing," Henry said, giving her a peck on the cheek. "The guests are sure to feel at home tonight."

"Mercy, I sure hope you're ready to work. That kitchen's fixin' to be busy," Abigail said.

Fetching an apron, Mercy met her at the stove.

"We've got stew in the stockpot and corn boiling over the fire out back. The pies are keeping warm over the stove, along with the biscuits. I've got cranberry sauce that can go out on the table now, and we've yet to mash the potatoes," Abigail said, out of breath by the time she finished.

Mercy took the potatoes and put them in another stockpot on the stove. The tavern smelled wonderful. Mercy admired Abigail. She always saw their patrons as guests, even the unruly ones, and did her best to make them feel at home. If there was a way to go above and beyond, she would find it. And Henry, for his part, was always quick to support her kind heart.

Around four-thirty, guests began to trickle into the tavern. Their oohs and ahhs could be heard all the way to the kitchen. Tonight, the guests were mostly officers and their favored subordinates, which meant that civil decorum would be the order of the evening, at least until they got deep in their cups.

A round of applause went up as Abigail and the boys began bringing out the seemingly endless dishes of food. The officers toasted Mrs. Abigail for her hospitality and cooking. There was much merriment and even singing as the night wore on. Mercy smiled and laughed as the officers told silly stories about one another and joked about the British in Boston.

Dessert brought about a fresh round of celebration, and it was beginning to become clear that the cider had also been a big hit.

Henry had wisely collected a fee from each guest for the night that would amply cover the tavern's investments. Mercy appreciated his business bearing. He was always fair in his dealings with others, and possessed the savvy to keep the tavern afloat, even in the troubled times.

As it neared closing time, it was even more obvious that the cider had been greatly enjoyed. Mercy hoped the redcoats wouldn't choose tomorrow to attack. If they did, it was unlikely there would be very many Continental officers up to the task. Henry helped the men get each other out the door, and the officers, along with their merriment, staggered off towards camp.

"That was a delightful evening, just delightful." Abigail beamed as Henry returned.

"You did well," Henry said. Then he chuckled, "Those officers sure are going to hear it tomorrow, might not see them back for a bit."

Mercy set the table for six, and sitting down to dinner, they each took stock of how much they had to be thankful for.

When it came to Abigail, she looked around the table and, taking David's hand, she said, "I'm thankful for our family, for the goodness of the Lord that brought you here, has kept us safe, and I believe will one day bring your Papa home. I know it may seem selfish of me to say it, but you'll forever occupy that place in my heart."

"And in mine," Henry added.

"Well, before I get all misty, we'd better eat," Abigail said.

That night, Mercy groaned as she lay in bed, she couldn't remember ever having eaten that much. Abigail's cooking really was toast worthy. She thought about what Abigail had said and about Papa. It was perplexing, being a part of two families, and yet they were. And if God had led them to this, then it was where they were supposed to be.

She wondered what life would be like when they got Papa back. What would happen to Henry and Abigail? Trying to figure it all out caused her head and heart to ache. At last, she conceded and decided she would let God work it all out—it was His idea after all. Satisfied with her decision, she was finally able to relax enough to fall asleep.

Chapter 14

December 1, 1775

This morning we woke up to snowflakes floating down from the sky. Some of them were as big as the button on my cloak and heavy. At first there wasn't much of a breeze, and they fell soft, like you'd expect them to in a fairy tale. By lunch, the wind picked up considerable, and the snow whipped around here and there, and made small piles in the corners of the buildings.

The general has kept the soldiers drilling even in the cold. They are looking right smart now in their formations. They seem to execute commands with ease as they turn this way and that. Benjamin heard from a couple of officers that the militia's enlistments will be up soon and that many of the soldiers will be heading back to their homes.

Benjamin also heard about a fort in New York that was defeated by a militia calling themselves the Green Mountain Boys. It *had a funny name, Ticonderoga. According to the officers, General Washington wants the cannons from the fort brought all the way to Cambridge. That trip would be three hundred miles through the wilderness. I can't imagine anyone going three hundred miles in winter. Why, on the especially bitter days, it's difficult to want to make the trek to the barn.*

Henry said that we would all go cut a Christmas tree this Sunday after the service. I do hope we can find the perfect one, not one that is too sparse, or too squatty, or leans to one side or the other. A sorry Christmas tree can throw off the balance of the entire room. There will be paper doll garlands to make, a star, and strings of popcorn and cranberries.

Christmas is the only thing that can bring light to the bitterness of winter, in my opinion. The smell of pine needles, sound of carolers, and giving gifts, oh, and hot cider, and hearing the story of Jesus' birth. It truly is the most wonderful time of the year.

Mercy Young, 13 years old.

―――

"Have mercy, Mercy," Abe whined as they passed up yet another nearly perfect spruce tree.

The six of them had been walking for over an hour along the river near the clearings, where the younger evergreens could be found. Henry and Abigail held hands, walking behind the troop of eager tree hunters. Benjamin carried a single man buck saw over his shoulder, ready to cut down whatever tree finally met Mercy's strict standards.

The ankle-deep snow afforded them one luxury, a sled. Henry had pulled it down from the rafters of the barn and added a little wax to the runners. It pulled like butter through the snow. Abe and David took turns giving each other rides as they went along. The sun warmed the day, causing the snow to stick to itself.

Out of nowhere, a snowball exploded between Benjamin's shoulders.

"Hey!" he said, whipping around.

Everyone stopped in their tracks. Benjamin dropped the saw and scooped up a mitt full of snow. He packed it together and launched it at a shocked Abe.

"It wasn't me!" Abe yelled, diving for cover.

Henry burst out laughing. "It was me!" he said with a mischievous grin.

Benjamin loaded up another snowball and sent it sailing in his direction. Abigail squealed and hid behind a tree as Abe loaded up a revenge shot at Benjamin. Snowballs flew in every direction, exploding on trees and bushes all around them.

"Take that!" Benjamin called out, landing a solid hit on Henry's thigh just before being tackled by Abe.

Scooping up an armload of snow, Henry hurled it at David, knocking him off his feet.

"Brothers," Benjamin declared nobly, "we must unite to vanquish this foe."

Seeing he was outnumbered; Henry dove for cover behind a bush as the three boys began their assault. A barrage of snowballs peppered his position—he was under siege. As soon as Henry popped up to return fire at one of the boys, the other two opened fire. He was left with no choice. Henry burst from the bush with a snowball in each hand. Like a professional marksman, he dropped Abe, then David and, rushing upon Benjamin, he tackled him in the snow.

David and Abe jumped on the pile, laughing and yelling insults as they wrestled with Henry. Abigail cheered for Henry and then the boys, and then Henry again. Abe and David had a leg each as Benjamin tried to pin a writhing Henry to the ground.

"I found it!"

The wrestling match stopped, and Henry stood up, his neck still in a headlock.

"I found it!" came Mercy's call again. She was standing only thirty yards away, staring admirably at a young spruce tree.

Gathering around, everyone listened as Mercy detailed the merits of the tree. "This one is the perfect shape from every side, nearly symmetrical. It hasn't got a noticeable lean, and although the height is a little much, we can cut it to size. It's fuller than most of the trees we've looked at, and if you look right here, there's a bird's nest for luck."

"It looks like all the others to me," said Abe, still brushing snow from his hair.

Mercy rolled her eyes.

"It's a lovely tree, Mercy," said Abigail.

"Did anyone see where I dropped that saw?" Benjamin asked.

"It's over near the sled," Abigail replied.

Henry held the tree steady as Benjamin cut it down. He had to lay on his side to get the proper angle, the boughs were thick right to the ground. When he finished, Henry and Abe carried the tree over to the sled, and using a bit of cordage, lashed it down.

It was getting on in the afternoon as they headed back to the wagon. The boys shivered in their wet clothes as they walked.

Sighing, Mercy removed her cloak and placed it over David's shoulders. "At least you gave as good as you got," she said, smiling.

At last, they reached the wagon and loaded the tree into the back. The boys rode with the tree while Mercy, Abigail, and Henry squeezed onto the buckboard. Sitting between Henry and Abigail, Mercy felt warm and safe. The search for the tree had been exhausting and, as the wagon swayed, she drifted off to sleep.

When she awoke, Henry was carrying her into the tavern. "Have a good sleep?" he asked. Mercy nodded.

The boys changed clothes, and they got a bite to eat before going to work on the tree. When it was all finished, Henry lifted David so that he could place the star Abigail had made on the top.

"It's perfect!" Mercy exclaimed.

After one last mug of hot cider, it was time for bed. Mercy's heart was full, and she couldn't remember a time when she felt more joy. Listening to the soft breathing of her exhausted brothers, Mercy committed the day to memory. One day, she hoped to tell Papa all about it.

Chapter 15

The snow from the day before had melted, leaving the town a dreadful mess. The ground was soggy, and the roofs dripped continuously. Mercy was dreading the night's clean up; mud had been tracked through the tavern everywhere. On top of that, the dreary weather seemed to drive folks into the tavern, looking for some warmth and a bit of cheer.

To make matters worse, Abigail was her usual jovial self, seeing only the Lord's blessings, and refusing to participate in Mercy's protest.

"If we can lift these tired souls up even a little bit, it's a blessing," she said.

"What about my tired soul?" grumbled Mercy.

"Well, aren't you full of vinegar," laughed Abigail.

"I don't see what there is to be so joyful about. We're likely to be up 'til all hours, scrubbing our fingers to a nub, just to get these floors looking decent. And tomorrow, we'll have to do it all over again," Mercy said.

"Well, that may be, child, but we could be those poor souls out there having to work and slave in the very mud they're draggin' in here. Instead, here we sit, nice and cozy near the stove, sipping cider as we tend the kitchen. I reckon there isn't a man amongst them who wouldn't gladly trade places, regardless of washin' the floors," Abigail replied.

"I doubt there's a man amongst them who'd know the first thing about tendin' the kitchen," quipped Mercy.

This brought about a fresh round of laughter from Abigail. "That may be, Mercy, that may very well be."

Just then, Henry came through the door from the tavern. "What are you two ladies laughing about?"

"Oh, Mercy's refusing to see any sunshine today on account of the floors," Abigail said bluntly.

"It's all part of the business," Henry said, returning from the back room with a barrel over his shoulder. "You've got to take the good with the bad, and learn to see that, as a whole, it's all a blessing." He walked back into the tavern.

"See," said Abigail. "Even Henry agrees with me."

Mercy huffed.

Suddenly, an explosion tremored through the tavern. It sounded somewhat like cannon fire, but less directed. The tavern went still for a moment, and when nothing happened, everyone returned to what they were doing. Abigail shrugged her shoulders and the two of them went back to work.

A full twenty minutes had passed when the back door of the tavern flew open. It was one of the doctor's assistants.

"Mrs. Abigail, you have to come quickly. There was a cannon burst at the camp and many soldiers are wounded. It's bad, and there are too many for us to treat. Please, hurry!" Without waiting for a reply, the assistant ran out the door.

"Mercy, fetch Henry and tell him we have to go. He'll understand. Go, now!"

Mercy found Henry and told him what the assistant had said. He said they would manage and told Mercy to go along too.

Abigail had already changed into a clean apron and was holding one for Mercy. "Let's go, Mercy!"

When they arrived at the doctor's, three men already lay on tables, two more still writhed in a wagon outside.

"We don't have any more room in here," said the doctor.

A trembling soldier, not older than fifteen, sat on the buckboard. Abigail turned to the boy and said, "Do you know where the tavern is?"

The soldier nodded.

"Take us there."

Mercy and Abigail climbed into the wagon, and the soldier cracked the reins. When they arrived, Henry took one look in the wagon and cleared out the tavern. A couple of the men who had been drinking helped carry the wounded soldiers inside and lay them on the tables. Abigail called for more light and the boys brought over lanterns.

"Mercy, get some rags boiling. Henry, get these men some ale. David, fetch my sewing needle and thread, and Benjamin, I'm gonna need water, a lot of water. Abe, bring me the scissors."

Everyone flew into action. Abigail cut the men's clothes off, revealing burns and deep gashes. Mercy returned with the rags and Abigail showed her how to clean the wounds. Carefully, they wiped the blood and mud from the men's bodies. Henry checked them for broken bones, relieved to find none. One of the men had a large piece of wood sticking out of his thigh. After Abe brought a thick wooden spoon, Abigail placed it in the man's mouth.

"Bite down, dear," she said.

As soon as the soldier complied, she nodded, and Henry jerked the piece of wood out. The soldier flinched hard and then went limp.

"Is he dead?" asked Abe.

"No, he just fell asleep," Abigail replied.

Abigail cleaned the wound with alcohol and, after running her needle through a flame, she sewed up the opening. Then she placed a bandage over it and tied it in place. She repeated this process several times on both patients and then she was done.

Abigail stood up and wiped her brow with the back of her hand. "They'll live, though I don't hold out much hope for the ones over at the doctor's. They were torn like some beast had had its way with them."

A short while later, another wagon pulled up outside the tavern, along with a rider on a white horse. There was a knock on the door, and Henry led the rider inside.

Abe gasped. "It's General Washington!"

The general spoke softly. He asked Abigail about the condition of his men and thanked them humbly for their services. He called in four more soldiers, who carried a couple of gurneys. Carefully, they laid the wounded soldiers on the gurneys and placed them in the wagon.

As the general turned to leave, Abigail caught his arm and asked, "What of the others?"

The general simply shook his head.

"I'm sorry for your loss," Abigail replied, and the general mounted his horse, tipped his hat one last time, and headed for the camp.

That night, as she scrubbed the mud mixed with blood from the floor, Mercy thought about the men who had died, and the others who had been so gravely injured. She decided that Abigail was right, there were many things worse than scrubbing mud, and she knew that any of those men would have gladly chosen to scrub the floor over dying in the mud. If that was the case, then scrubbing the floor really was something to be thankful for.

Chapter 16

December 4, 1775

Mr. Hadley stopped by earlier today to bring us the sad news that one of the boys Abigail stitched up died of a fever brought on by infection. The other soldier is faring much better and looks to make a full recovery. Abigail accepted the news with all the grace I have come to expect, though it was one of the few times I've witnessed her joy fade. She spent the rest of the day uncharacteristically quiet and reflective. This war has a way of wearing down the soul if one stays too close to it for too long.

Most days the war just seems like it'll stay this way forever, the British in Boston, and the Continentals surrounding them. We hear shots every now and again, though we've become so accustomed to it that I rarely flinch anymore. I keep hoping that one day, I'll wake up and the British will have given up and left, leaving Papa on the wharf. Henry says they have too much pride to leave and just enough sense not to attack.

The boys checked the snares again yesterday. It seems that clever coywolf has moved in and is content on letting us catch its dinner. Mr. Hadley said he'll teach us how to catch him too as soon as he can spare the time. Mr. Hadley knows how to tan the fur and said that, if we catch one, he'll make me a scarf. I've never owned a real fur before.

In the morning, after chores of course, the boys and I are going fishing at a deep pool Benjamin and Abe found. A beaver has stopped up the water with a dam and the water is deeper than a man and crystal clear. Benjamin said they could see schools of trout longer than a hatchet handle just waiting to be caught. Abigail discovered a sack of grain in the storeroom that was spoiled and full of grubs, so Benjamin asked her if we could have it for bait. If there's anything positive about these primitive circumstances, it's fishing.

Mercy Young, 13 years old.

The Youngs completed their chores in record time, gathered up the fishing canes they had used during the summer, and the sack of spoiled grain. The day was cold, but the combination of the sun's rays and the protection of the ravine made it bearable. Benjamin and Abe led the band through the woods along the creek's edge. It was quite steep at some points and Mercy had to cling to nearby tree branches to keep from slipping in.

At last, they reached the pool. Just as Benjamin had described, a beaver dam ran from one shore to the other, creating a deep circular pool of slowly swirling water. He had also been right about the fish; Mercy could see their dark silhouettes darting here and there.

Benjamin handed out the canes and opened the sack. It took a little digging, but the grubs were plentiful, and soon everyone was baited up.

"Me first!" said David, swinging his line out over the water. His grub had no more than brushed the surface of the water when a large spotted trout took it and made a run for the bottom of the pool.

"Get 'em, David!" yelled Abe.

David's cane bent hard as the fish dashed back and forth. Benjamin rushed over to help him, and together they horsed the fish ashore.

"Would you look at that!" Benjamin said, ruffling David's hair. "It's nearly as long as your arm." Benjamin slid the fish onto some twine and tied it to a nearby tree.

Mercy didn't delay. She swung her line out into the creek near where the water entered the pool. It only danced in the current for a moment before another trout took it. She set the hook, and the battle was on.

A shout went up near the beaver dam as Abe battled yet another trout. Benjamin re-baited David's hook, and they joined the fray. Abe laughed maniacally as he lifted a good four-pound trout from the water. Mercy drug another to shore while Benjamin and David were being equally successful.

"We're gonna run out of grubs at this rate!" laughed Benjamin.

Mercy loved seeing her brother so excited. Benjamin had taken responsibility for his family the day their father had been captured, and they had made it this far because of him. He tended to be on such alert while watching out for them that he didn't allow himself to enjoy things too much. He deserved this.

"You found a real good spot, Ben," Mercy said.

They re-baited their hooks and went at it again. Near the dam, on the far side of the creek, a giant trout leaped from the water.

"Did you see that thing!" cried Benjamin.

"I think I can still see it," said Abe. "There in that eddy, just sittin' there."

Benjamin swung his rod out as far as it would reach and dropped his bait in the water. It landed only a couple feet from the fish, but it made no effort to eat the grub. He tried again, this time, his bait landed just behind the fish. It made a slight flash as his line entered the water, but still no interest. Benjamin pulled his line in, disappointed.

"I think I'll have to go out on the dam," he said.

"I don't think you should," warned Mercy. "How do you know it'll hold you?"

"It's holdin' back all this water, Mercy, beavers are good at this sort of thing," he said, as he carefully made his way out onto the dam.

Reaching the halfway point, he was close enough for his cane to reach. Getting a good footing, he swung the line into the eddy a couple of feet ahead of the giant fish. The tiny grub swirled and bobbed in the current. Mercy and the boys held their breath as the grub neared the fish's head. Then, in a flash of scales, the grub was gone.

Mercy watched as Benjamin dug his heels in and set the hook. The lazy fish exploded from its resting spot with all the fury of a raging bull. It darted straight for the deepest part of the pool while Benjamin fought to keep the furious fish out of the protruding branches of the dam. Then the fish switched directions and bolted for the shore, causing Benjamin to lose his balance. He shifted his feet to catch himself, but ended up tripping on a branch.

"Benjamin!" Mercy shrieked as he tumbled into the pool.

Benjamin came sputtering to the surface, fighting franticly to swim through the frigid water in his soaking wet clothes.

Abe grabbed his cane and swung it out to Benjamin. "Grab it! I'll pull you in!" he shouted.

Benjamin did as he was told, and together, Mercy and Abe pulled him to shore. Benjamin shook violently as he stood.

"M-m-maybe t-t-that wasn't such a g-g-good idea," he chattered.

"We have to get you home," Mercy said.

They started up the hill, Abe helping Benjamin, Mercy carrying the fish, and David hauling the canes. They made it only a third of the way when Benjamin's legs gave out and he sunk into the wet leaves, trembling. Dropping the fish, Mercy rushed to his side, his color was fading to a sickly pale.

"We have to keep going," she said frantically. "Abe, put his arm around your shoulder, I'll take the other."

They managed to make it halfway home before losing their footing and dropping him again.

"This is bad, Abe, this is really bad," Mercy said, trying not to panic. She unbuttoned her cloak and threw it over Benjamin. "Abe, you have to run and get help, we'll stay here with him and try to keep him warm."

Abe nodded his head and took off up the hill.

David looked at Mercy, and then unbuttoned his coat and laid it over Benjamin's legs.

"Here David, take his hand like this and rub it between yours, like this," said Mercy, rubbing Benjamin's hand. "Feel that I' warm? Now, keep that up."

"M-m-mercy, I-I-I'm startin' t-t-to feel a little funny," Benjamin said, his teeth chattering. "M-m-my arms a-a-and l-l-legs aren't workin'."

"You're gonna be alright in just a minute. Abe went to fetch Henry and they're gonna be back here before you know it."

"T-t-that was a b-b-big fish, wasn't it?"

"It was a beauty." She smiled at him. "Not as big as my catfish, of course, but a big fish nonetheless."

Benjamin began to laugh, but it turned to coughing.

"Mercy, do you think Papa will be upset that I got all wet?" Benjamin asked, closing his eyes.

"Benjamin, Papa's with the Brit—" She stopped and looked at him. He'd stopped shivering, his breathing had slowed, and his words were slurred.

"Benjamin?"

He didn't respond. She shook him. "Ben!"

He opened his eyes, but immediately they began to close.

"Benjamin, you have to fight it. Stay awake!" she pleaded. "David, run to the top of the hill and see if you can see them!" Mercy commanded.

"Benjamin Young! You have to stay with me!" She shook him again and again.

His eyes opened and closed slowly, he mumbled something unintelligible and then closed his eyes again.

"I see them!" yelled David.

Mercy slapped Benjamin hard in the face. "Ben, they're almost here! Wake up, Benjamin!" And she slapped him again.

Above her, Mercy heard Henry running and sliding through the leaves, Abe on his heels. Reaching Mercy, Henry scooped up Benjamin.

"He won't wake up!" Mercy cried.

Henry hefted Benjamin in his arms and began to fight his way up the hill. "He'll be alright, Mercy, we have to get him to the fire."

When they reached the top of the hill, Henry rested, momentarily catching his breath. From his arms, they heard a faint voice. "A-A-Abe, don't forget the fish."

Abe squeezed his hand. "I'll get 'em, Ben." Abe tore off back down the hill and fetched the stringer.

Henry caught his wind, and they took off again at a trot for the tavern.

Abigail called to them as they reached the yard, "Bring him in, bring him in. I have the stove all ready and blankets."

Together, Henry and Abigail stripped off Benjamin's wet clothes and dried him off with towels. They wrapped him in a thick wool blanket and Henry sat with him in his lap by the fire.

"Lord have mercy, you children are going to be the death of me," Abigail said, wiping tears from her eyes. "Jesus, bring him 'round," she prayed.

By and by, Benjamin's color returned. His skin flushed with the heat of the stove and his breathing became strong and steady. At last, he opened his eyes and looked about. Abigail breathed a sigh of relief.

"Do you have any idea what you just did to me?!" she said, pounding her chest with her fist. "You've always been the responsible one. Why on earth would you do a fool thing like that? I don't know how I'd live if I lost you today." She rushed over and threw her arms around him.

Benjamin hugged her back awkwardly. "I'm sorry, ma'am, it was a really big fish," he whispered.

"That may be, but I wouldn't trade you for all the fish in the world. So please, never risk yourself for something so small again," she whispered back.

That night, after the tavern was closed, they feasted on fish stories and fish fillets, thankful to have survived another day.

Chapter 17

After Benjamin's accident, the rest of the week went by smoothly. Benjamin had recovered in a couple of days, though Abigail was still getting over it. She gave a speech every time one of the Youngs wanted to go anywhere that wasn't in sight of the tavern. Henry seemed to think the lesson was learned. Besides that, he had a dozen near-death stories of his own from his youth and he was still standing.

"It's a part of life," he had said.

To which Abigail replied, "Right up until you're dead."

By Sunday, things had settled down a bit. Reverend Greene's sermon was all about casting your cares on the Lord, and how He sees the sparrows that fall. Abigail came to tears and everyone knew she was thinking about Benjamin.

After the service, Mr. Hadley dropped by. His limp was less noticeable now, and at times he walked without a cane at all.

"I hear ya had a brush with death," he said, patting Benjamin on the back.

"It was nothin'," Benjamin shrugged.

"Nothin', my foot!" said Abigail. "You were nearly to the pearly gates when Henry brought you in."

Benjamin blushed.

"Well, if I had me an acre for every near-death experience I've had, why, I'd own the new world," Mr. Hadley said, slapping his knee.

"It's a wonder there are any men left on earth after all the near-death tales I've heard this week. The good Lord must be wearing out angels just to keep enough of you alive to sustain the population," Abigail fumed.

Mr. Hadley just chuckled. "Well, the reason I stopped over was to see about helping ya'll catch that coywolf. That's if it's alright with you, ma'am."

"Please?" begged David.

"Be back for dinner," Abigail said, throwing up her hands.

David threw his arms around her and gave her a hug. "Thank you, Mrs. Abigail."

"Oh, get going or you'll be late I' back."

Benjamin led the band to the snares where the coywolf had helped itself to every rabbit caught for the last week.

Mr. Hadley studied the scene. Pointing to a soft bit of mud with his cane, he said, "It's a fare-sized coywolf. That's a good track. The ol' boy is getting used to you feedin' him."

Picking a snare with a half-eaten rabbit in it, he showed the Youngs how to use fallen branches and brush to create a funnel that would direct the coywolf to the snare from the direction they desired. Next, he scoured the area for a heavy log until he found the perfect one. It was about five feet long and at least ten inches in diameter. It was a hard wood, and heavy.

After rolling the log into position in front of the snare, he gathered three hardwood sapling sticks. After some carving, he fashioned them into a crude figure 4. The Youngs sat back in wonder.

"Benjamin, I'm gonna need you to hold these sticks exactly like this. I'm gonna lift that log and set it gently on the top of that stick," said Mr. Hadley.

Benjamin nodded, a little unsure. Mercy thought there was no chance the strange-looking number 4 would be able to hold the log, but Benjamin did as he was told.

"One, two, three . . ." Mr. Hadley groaned as he lifted one end of the log. Reaching the height of the stick, he gently placed it on top. "Okay, Ben, you can let go now."

Benjamin let go and slid away from the log. Mr. Hadley steadied it for a moment, and then slowly let go. To Mercy's surprise, the log remained perched at the top of the stick.

"Wow!" Mercy breathed in wonder.

Grabbing another stick, Mr. Hadley said, "Gather round. When your coywolf comes lookin' for his midnight snack, he'll smell the rabbit, circle the trap, and come in from the front just like we want him to. He'll approach the trap cautiously, but he's succeeded in stealing your rabbits so many times before, he'll enter through this space here between the log and the sticks. When his body brushes this stick..." He gave the cross member of the figure four a slight nudge, and the log dropped to the ground with a powerful thud.

The Youngs jumped back in surprise and applauded. Laughing, Mr. Hadley took a bow.

"We'll get him, for sure!" cried Abe.

"You're full of tricks," said Mercy.

"My father was a good trapper. There wasn't a critter alive who could outfox him," Mr. Hadley replied.

Mr. Hadley walked them through setting the trap up again, and when everything was in place, they added a little camouflage and headed off for the tavern.

The following morning, the kitchen was all abuzz with speculation about whether or not there would be a coywolf in the trap. Henry thought the idea was genius and decided that he would accompany the kids as well. Abigail, on the other hand, was torn between feeling pity for the coywolf, and hoping that the bugger was trapped so that she could get some rabbits for stew again.

Mercy didn't like the killing part either, but she understood that all of life is a struggle of life and death. The coywolf ate rabbits, wolves would catch and kill coywolves, and so on. Even the plants competed for the sun, shading their competition to death if they were able. And yet, somehow, God had found a way to make it all work in balance.

After breakfast, the five of them set off for the woods. The night had left a heavy frost on the ground so that the grass glittered in the sunlight. The twigs and remaining leaves on the trees were cloaked in a beautiful white fuzz. Their breath floated lazily in the air as they walked. Mercy's ears and nose tingled with the cold.

Mercy caught up with Henry and snuggled under his arm as they walked. The leaves crunched loudly under their feet as they reached the woods. To their surprise, not only did the first snare have a rabbit in it, but it was intact. Carefully removing the rabbit, Benjamin tossed it to David. Then he set the snare again. The second snare was empty, but still set. The third snare is where they had set the coywolf deadfall.

"We're getting close," said Benjamin.

Mercy tightened her grip on Henry's hand in anticipation. As they rounded a small bend, Mercy could see through the leafless trees that the log Mr. Hadley had set on top of the sticks was not where he had left it. The brush they used as a funnel obscured her view of the trap itself.

"The log is missing!" cried David in excitement.

"I think we'd best take it easy," Henry suggested. "If there's a coywolf in there, it may only be injured and could be quite aggressive."

The five of them crept up to the trap, Henry peering over the brush first. Sighing admirably, he said, "It's safe, you can take a look."

Following Benjamin and the boys around the front of the funnel, Mercy saw the coywolf lying dead, the heavy log resting just behind its shoulders.

"Whoa! It worked!" exclaimed Abe.

"That explains the rabbit in the first snare," said Benjamin.

Abe hopped over the log and, using a small twig, lifted the coywolf's lip.

"Look at those teeth!"

Sneaking up behind him, Henry yelled, "Raaar!"

Abe jumped clean over the brush and ran a full ten yards before stopping. "You nearly gave me a heart attack!" he yelled, pelting Henry with one pinecone, and then another.

"Okay, okay, I'm sorry," laughed Henry, "I couldn't resist."

Abe hit him with a final pinecone before accepting his apology.

"Well, I guess we'd better get him out of there," Henry said. "Benjamin, you slide him out by the back legs while I lift the log." Henry moved into position. "One, two, three . . ." Henry lifted the log and Benjamin slid the coywolf back with ease.

Once the coywolf was free, they took time to admire it. It had beautiful blond hair on its belly that faded into a mixed grey pattern on its back. Its tail was thick and bushy, and on its head were two erect, soft, furry ears. All things considered; it wasn't much more than a medium-sized dog. Mercy felt pity for the creature. Under any other circumstances, she would have been happier to let the coywolf live. But they needed rabbits for food, and that meant they couldn't afford the coywolf's thievery, and so, like the rest of nature, they had to compete, and this time, the coywolf had lost.

"Well, should we go show Abigail?" Henry asked, hoisting frozen the coywolf onto his shoulders.

As they walked back to the tavern, Mercy thought about the bittersweet feeling of catching the coywolf. It was somehow different from catching the rabbits. The coywolf wasn't food; it was competition. It was a struggle, and the Youngs had prevailed. And again, there was that stirring, that connection to the woods, that knowledge that can only come from being a part of it and joining the struggle. Again, she wanted more of it.

When they reached the tavern, Abigail was out hanging the laundry on the line.

"Looks like you caught the brute."

"And a rabbit," David said, holding up his prize.

"What are you planning on doing with it?" she asked.

"Mr. Hadley said he'd tan it for me," said Mercy.

"We'll have to leave it buried in some dry leaves on the north side of the shed until he can come and fetch it. Don't want it to thaw before then," Henry said.

Abe and David helped Henry gather leaves to insulate the coywolf while Benjamin and Mercy got busy with the work of the day. She couldn't wait to write this adventure down in her diary and share it with Papa one day. She thought it was only proper that they kept the coywolf's hide. It would remind her always of the struggle, of its cunning in taking their rabbits, and in the end, its foolish confidence that led to its death. It would remind her that it had lived, that the woods were full of fascinating creatures that all lived and died in the great struggle for balance.

Chapter 18

December 15, 1775

Today was Mama's birthday. Every year I find myself a little down on this day., I still can hear her laugh and see her smile if I try hard enough. I often wonder if she's looking down on us, watching us in all our adventuring. I hope she knows I'm doing my best to keep up the boys' schooling, though with the work at the tavern, it's less than perfect. I think she would like Henry and Abigail, and Mr. Hadley too, though he is a bit rough around the edges. I know she must see Papa; the Lord wouldn't separate them like that.

It's only ten days 'til Christmas, and the reverend has had a little choir practicing carols. Abigail and I go and sing when we can. It's hard for me to comprehend why God would want to send Jesus to a place He knew would treat him so terrible to save sinners. As far as I can tell, mankind has an awful habit of making our own *hell to live in. I guess that just lends authority to the fact that we need a shepherd.*

Speaking of needing a shepherd, Abe and Benjamin snuck off back to the beaver dam to take another shot at catching that big trout. Abigail nearly tanned their hides when she found out. I've never seen her so upset. Henry had to risk his good standing in order to defend those two fools. I was feeling rather hot myself over the whole thing, but I think Abigail did enough scolding for the both of us. Abe was near to tears by the time she was done, and Benjamin looked like he had seen a ghost. Even so, I doubt it'll be the last time.

Mercy Young, 13 years old.

Saturday morning at breakfast, Henry announced that he would be leaving on a two-day journey to Charlestown, South Carolina, for supplies. Abigail said nothing, but she seemed apprehensive.

Henry asked Mercy if she would accompany him.

"If Mrs. Abigail can survive without me for today," she said, looking questioningly at Abigail.

"I'll be alright, child, you go along."

Abe put up a protest on why Mercy got to go and not him, but Henry just insisted it would be better this way.

Henry had prepared the team before breakfast and, as soon as they were finished, they were off. Mercy loved going on trips with Henry. There were always so many things to see, and the scenery was beautiful. Henry always let her drone on and on about the beauty and curiosity of it all, something the boys never appreciated.

The day was particularly chilly, so Abigail had sent a couple of blankets with them; one to throw over their shoulder and one for their laps. The roads were muddy, causing the horses' hooves to make a grotesque sound as they slopped along. Mercy wondered what it would feel like to have that kind of mud between her toes.

"Mr. Henry? Why aren't we going to New York like we usually do?" asked Mercy.

"Because the supplies we're picking up aren't in New York."

"What supplies are we getting, then?"

Henry thought for a moment before answering. "We're on a secret mission for General Washington."

"A secret mission?!" Mercy exclaimed.

"Shhh, you need to keep quiet about it!"

"Why?"

"Because not all the colonists support the Continentals. There are many Loyalists who will do harm to those they feel are disloyal to the Crown. People call them Tories," Henry answered.

"What if they try to do us harm?"

"I'll protect you."

"So, what's our mission?" Mercy asked excitedly.

"We are meeting with a man, a gunsmith to be exact, who has a stockpile of weapons and powder to get to the Continentals. The problem is the Tories keep attacking the Continental wagons sent to fetch them. That's why the general asked if we could use our wagon, and the alibi of fetching supplies, to transport the weapons back to Cambridge."

"What do the Tories look like?" Mercy asked.

"Like you and me."

"How will we know them, then?" she asked, perplexed.

"That's why we have to keep it quiet," Henry said with a smile.

The whole thing felt so exhilarating that Mercy had a hard time not talking about it. A secret mission, and for the general, no less. She eyed every person they passed on the road, wondering if they could be a Tory. She practiced being inconspicuous, not looking for too long or too little. She laughed at random and slapped Henry's arm as they passed another wagon.

"What's so funny?" asked Henry.

"Just play along," she whispered, laughing again.

Henry shook his head and chuckled.

Around noon, they pulled the wagon to the side of the road, and Henry let the team chew on what grass and weeds were there. Mercy took out the basket of sandwiches Abigail had packed and climbed out of the wagon to stretch her legs. As they ate, a beautiful carriage rolled past with a dark-skinned man driving it. In the carriage sat a beautiful young woman in a splendid pink and blue dress.

"Is that man a slave?" Mercy asked.

"I suspect so," said Henry.

"He must be a terribly long way from his home."

"They come from across the ocean, ships loaded with hundreds of them carry them here from Africa. I've seen the ships unload, and it's a pitiful sight," Henry said.

"Papa said that slavin' isn't right," said Mercy.

"Sounds like your papa and I have a lot in common," said Henry with a smile.

"Do you think they'll ever be free?"

"Someday," Henry said. "Someday, the world will grow up and we'll treat all people as equals."

"I hope so," said Mercy, watching the carriage disappear around the bend.

Finishing their lunch, they continued on until at last, around suppertime, they pulled into Charlestown. Henry pulled the wagon up to the general store and jumped out.

"Come along, Mercy. Let's get some supplies."

Inside the general store, Mercy saw shelves and shelves of every kind of thing a body could want. There were fabrics and dishes, shovels and garden tools, flour and beans, tools and twine, and at the counter . . . candies.

"You want some?" Henry asked, not missing her wishful expression.

"Yes, please," said Mercy, eyes wide with anticipation.

"Add a few candies for the girl," Henry said, handing money to the gruff-looking man behind the counter.

It took several trips in and out before Henry had all the flour, salt pork, beans, and other supplies loaded in the wagon. The wagon was so full, in fact, Mercy didn't know where the "other" supplies were going to fit.

Henry climbed aboard and handed Mercy her candy. "Now, we wait."

And wait they did. Mercy was about to die of boredom as the sun dipped behind the horizon. Finally, as night fell, Henry snapped the reins, and the team lurched forward at a slow walk. As they neared the edge of town, a man walked out of a house carrying a lantern.

"Are you Henry?" the man asked.

Henry nodded and got out of the wagon. Mercy watched as the men exchanged words. Together, they unloaded Henry's supplies, and then, to Mercy's surprise, Henry lifted the boards that made up the bed of the wagon, revealing a second bottom an entire foot below the false bottom. The man with the lantern nodded approvingly. He led Henry to a shed behind the house and together they carried several crates and barrels to the wagon. Mercy could tell the crates were heavy based on all the grunting. They returned to the shed and brought out several shiny new muskets, their barrels gleaming in the moonlight.

"That's it," the man said.

Henry replaced the false floor, and the men piled the supplies for the tavern on top.

"Godspeed," said the man.

Henry shook his hand and climbed into the wagon. With a snap of the reins, the horses were moving again.

"There's an inn near the general store. We'll stay there tonight and head out at first light," Henry said.

Mercy was so excited. First, this was a secret mission, then, there was a secret compartment in the wagon, and not only that, but she would also be staying in an inn! She was absolutely giddy, despite the cold. When Henry pulled up the wagon, a dark-skinned man met them. Henry instructed him in the care of the team and slipped him a silver coin. The man thanked Henry with a bow and led the team and wagon to the rear of the inn.

Henry held the door for Mercy, and she walked into the inn with her chin held just a tad higher than normal. They entered a large, well-lit room, where a bald man standing behind a counter welcomed them.

"I need a room," said Henry.

"Would you like a bath as well?"

"No, the room is enough," said Henry.

"Ohhh," Mercy groaned.

"Ahh, I guess we'll take the bath," Henry chuckled.

"One room and a bath," the man said. He rang a little bell and a woman in an apron appeared.

"Follow me," she said softly.

She led them down a hallway past several doors before she stopped. "This 'ns yours," she said. "I'll be back to draw up your bath presently."

Henry opened the door and motioned for Mercy to enter. The room was larger than their room at the tavern; the bed was large with thick blankets, and two lanterns hung on the wall flanking the bed. A separate smaller room contained a bathtub, washbasin, and a large-framed mirror.

"It's beautiful," Mercy said.

"I'll let you have the bed," said Henry. "I'm afraid it'd be too soft for me."

"Really?" Mercy said, jumping on the bed. She sunk into the down comforter, sighing loudly. "This is the best adventure ever."

The woman reappeared and began filling up the bath. After several trips, the bath was full, and Mercy climbed in. At first the water was so hot it took her breath away, but she acclimated to it. It was her first bath in a tub she could stretch her legs in, and it felt heavenly. By and by, she drifted off.

A knock at the door shook her from her sleep. "Mercy, are you alright in there? It's been forty-five minutes and we should get some rest."

"Yes, I'm just getting out now," she replied, rushing to give truth to her words.

Mercy opened the door to see Henry holding a beautiful pink dress. She moved her hand to her mouth involuntarily.

"I, uhh, saw you staring at it in the store and, well, do you like it?" Henry asked.

"It's wonderful," Mercy breathed out.

"Good, I thought you could wear it on the ride home. It will be Sunday, after all."

Giving him a big hug, she let out a little squeal. "Thank you, Mr. Henry!"

That night, Mercy slept like a queen. In the morning, she donned her new dress and spun in front of the mirror several times.

"You look beautiful," Henry said.

Mercy watched curiously as Henry hid a silver coin under the pillow.

"What's that for?"

"When the young maid who filled your bath cleans our room, she'll find the coin. It's a way of saying thank you."

Mercy walked out of the inn with all the pomp of a proper fashionable woman, even going as far as to take Henry's arm. He helped her into the wagon, and they headed for home.

There were very few people on the road on account of it being Sunday. Mercy thought it clever they had chosen that day for their secret mission. They were almost out of South Carolina when a small band of men met them on horseback.

"Whoa, there," said a powdered wig-wearing man. "Where are you headed?"

"We're headed for Boston," said Henry. "We run a tavern near there."

The man eyed him suspiciously. "Would you mind stepping down from your wagon?"

"Why would I do that?" asked Henry.

"Why, to avoid any trouble, sir," said the man with a sneer. "We've got word that the Continentals are smuggling munitions out of the South to Washington besieging our countrymen at Boston. I'm sure you wouldn't mind us taking a look in the name of the king."

Henry shook his head, and taking Mercy by the hand, climbed down. Several of the men climbed off their horses and began going through the contents of the wagon. Mercy's heart slammed against the walls of her chest, and she squeezed Henry's hand tightly.

"Looks like you're preparing for quite the Christmas feast," said the man with the wig. "What's your name, pretty girl?"

Mercy slid behind Henry.

The man in the wig laughed gutturally. "Shy one, isn't she?"

Mercy peered out from under Henry's arm just as one of the men started stomping on the floor of the wagon. She felt Henry tense. Mercy's mind raced; they were going to be found out.

She burst out from behind Henry. "How dare you destroy my papa's wagon like that! With no regard for the good people who will be eating that food, and the blood, sweat, and tears he and Mama put into buildin' our tavern. You're no more than cowardly brutes. This is no better treatment than what we got at the hands of the Continentals!" Mercy said, fuming. "Is this how you treat a Loyalist and his daughter, and on the Lord's day, of all things?"

The man in the white wig stared at her in shocked disbelief. "Not so shy after all," he said with a loud guffaw, slapping his thigh. "You're gonna have your hands full with that one, sir." Then, turning to the other men, he said, "Let them be, boys, they've got a long ride ahead of them, yet."

Henry and Mercy mounted the wagon, and the man in the wig tipped his hat. "For your loyalty, sir."

Henry snapped the reins, and the wagon started off. The two of them rode in silence until they were far away from the men on horses.

"I'm sorry, Henry," Mercy said.

"Sorry for what?" asked Henry. "You saved us as sure as I'm sittin' here." He pulled her close. "I'm sorry I got you into this, Mercy, I thought just having you along would've been deterrent enough."

"I don't think we should tell Mrs. Abigail about it," Mercy said, biting her lip.

Henry snorted, then laughed. "Yes, that goes without saying. I don't think either of us would survive that tongue lashing."

"At least General Washington will be pleased," said Mercy.

"Let's hope he doesn't ask us to make that trip again."

The sun was dipping behind the horizon when they pulled into the yard. Everyone came running from the tavern together, all of them talking at once. Abigail threw her arms around them both.

"Thank the good Lord you're alright. I've been near to tears with worry all day. Did you run into any trouble?"

"Nothing Mercy couldn't have handled on her own," Henry said cheerfully.

"I see you've been spoilin' her," Abigail said with a wink. "Go on, Mercy, give us a twirl.

Mercy spun in a circle.

"That looks right lovely on you, Mercy," she said.

Mercy reached into the wagon and pulled out the candy. "For you, boys."

Abe took the small paper bag and made a run for it, David and Benjamin at his heels.

"Oh, good heavens," laughed Abigail. She took Henry and Mercy by the hand and led them into the tavern. "Now, tell me all about your trip."

"Get 'em, Dave!" yelled Abe.

Dave set the hook with a powerful yank that sent the poor creature blasting from the water. David fell backwards with the

December 23, 1775

Tomorrow is Christmas Eve! The tavern has been transformed into an enchanted Christmas Hall. Abigail and I made wreathes from pine boughs, the boys made paper angels and snowflakes, and we've set out extra candles. Abigail says that we will celebrate Christmas tomorrow because it's Sunday and the tavern won't be open. Henry's been acting rather strange lately. He makes secret trips out to the shed every now and again, but when I ask him about it, he always winks and says, "It's for General Washington."

Benjamin heard some officers talking about the cannons from Fort Ticonderoga. A Colonel Knox is bringing them by sled all the way to Cambridge. They said the cannons will be just what the Continentals need to break the stalemate and drive the British out of the colonies. I sure hope they are right.

The weather has been colder and wetter than ever, and the doctor has had his hands full with the fever. The morale of the soldiers seems lower than ever, I reckon most of them are missing home terribly.

Conditions must be worse in Boston. Henry said they are using the wood from the houses damaged in the bombardments to keep warm. I don't think anyone imagined the siege could last this long. General Washington has kept the Continentals drilling for weeks now, by this time they must be able to follow the commands in their sleep, I surely could.

I hope and pray with all my heart that the war ends soon, though I've never been a prisoner before, I can't imagine anyone holding out much hope after so long a time.

I wonder if Jesus didn't choose the dreariest time of the year to be born because He knew that in times like this, folks would need something to look forward to, something to give them hope.

Mercy Young, 13 years old.

"Mercy, Mercy, wake up!" David yelled. "It's Christmas Eve!"

Groaning, Mercy rolled over. "David, this is the one day I don't have to get up with that drummer."

"But it's Christmas Eve, Mercy."

"It'll still be Christmas Eve in an hour . . ." Mercy moaned.

"Oh, come on, Mercy," said Benjamin, "Abigail made rolls with brown sugar glaze on top. They taste better warm."

"All right. Give me a minute to collect myself and I'll be simple as that.

Abigail showed Mercy how to batter the fish with flour and salt and fry them in the pan. The smell soon filled the tavern sweet rolls, but there was also a glazed ham, eggs with cheese, and fresh milk. The kitchen smelled divine.

"Good morning, Mercy," Abigail said in her normal cheery voice.

"Good morning, Mrs. Abigail. It smells wonderful."

Henry came through the door, shivering. "It's a cold one out there. I had to drop a load of wood off for the reverend. The chapel is going to be a might chilly on account of this driving wind."

Giving Abigail a peck on the cheek as he passed, Henry made his way to his seat at the head of the table. "Everyone, take your seats, I'm starving and this feast demands my attention," he said cheerfully.

The boys ran to their seats and Mercy took hers. Henry said grace and they dug in. Abe was on his third slice of ham and reaching for a fourth when Abigail caught him by the hand.

"Abraham, finish the one you're working on first," she chided.

Abe tucked the remaining corners of the ham into his mouth, causing his cheeks to bulge, and then reached again. Abigail caught him by his hand again. "Chew it up." Abe did as he was told, then slowly, he reached again.

"Go ahead," Abigail said.

Mercy blushed with embarrassment; Abe was a barbarian.

After breakfast, they endured a passionate sermon about the dreadful sin of man, and the love of God that moved Him to come to our rescue. Reverend Greene talked about the foolishness of man that they would have the scriptures of their day memorized, and yet fail to recognize the Son of God. Then he said that mankind still fails to see the goodness of God in our everyday circumstances. Mercy didn't want to agree with the reverend, but she knew he was right. She set her mind to do better.

The boys skipped home after the service without regard for the biting wind. In truth, Mercy wanted to join them, but she knew it wouldn't be proper for a woman to skip home in her new dress, especially given the muddy conditions. Abigail joyfully hummed carols as they walked, and even Henry seemed to be enjoying himself, as he should, with a pretty lady on each arm.

At the tavern, the air was thick with excitement. Henry played it off as though he hadn't noticed it, going about his Sunday as he always did with a smoke of his pipe while reading a book. Abigail and Mercy baked gingersnap cookies with sugar on top, while David and Abe wrestled on the floor. Benjamin patiently whittled a stick, flicking the shavings into the fire.

Mercy had to hide her surprised laugh when it was Abigail who broke first.

"Henry, can't we just give them their gifts now?" she pleaded.

Benjamin's knife froze, and the boys stopped wrestling.

Henry took a long draw on his pipe. "We agreed on after dinner," he said coolly.

"How is anyone supposed to endure this amount of anxiety?" she complained.

"Be anxious for nothing . . ." he said, taking another draw.

"I've dreamed of a Christmas like this my whole life. Won't you give me this one small pleasure?"

Henry stood up from his chair, grinning. "I know you have, love." He looked around the room at all the excited faces. "I suppose we could break from our newly formed tradition just this once."

A chorus of cheers went up.

Abigail had each of them sit around the tree while Henry and Benjamin brought in the gifts from the shed. Abe and David oohed and awed as they placed each package under the tree, and Abigail hung the stockings in front of the fireplace. Mercy couldn't remember being so happy. She was warm and safe, the tavern smelled of ginger snaps and cider, she was surrounded by people who loved her, and everywhere, there was merriment. At least for the moment, there was no war, no suffering or loneliness, no fear. There was only joy.

Henry handed a gift to each one of them and, after taking his seat next to Abigail, he said, "Go ahead, open them."

David went first, tearing off the wrapping paper with both hands. Inside, he found a box full of little lead soldiers. Next was Abe. Under his wrapping paper was a model naval ship and his own small box of lead soldiers to man it. Then came Mercy. She received two new books, one of which was The Adventures of Roderick Random. She had been longing for some new books and hugged them both to her chest. Lastly, Benjamin opened his gift. It was long and heavy-looking, and he peeled away the paper to reveal a Kentucky Long Rifle, complete with powder horn and pouches with ball ammo and patches.

Benjamin looked up at Henry quickly, like he thought maybe he had received the gun by mistake, but Henry was sitting back in his chair wearing a big grin.

"Thank you!" Benjamin said, stroking the barrel, a bit beside himself.

They all thanked Henry and Abigail with hugs and kisses. Abigail couldn't help herself and let the tears of joy fall.

Then Henry spoke up, "There's one more." He reached into his pocket and pulled out a small envelope and handed it to

Mercy. "It's from General Washington, for your part in our secret mission."

Mercy took the envelope. It was heavy for its size, and lumpy. She lifted the flap and reached inside. Inside was a fine silver chain necklace with a small, single pearl suspended from it.

"Oh! It's beautiful!" she gasped.

Abigail got up and walked over to her. She held out her hand and Mercy placed the delicate chain into it. "Turn around," she said sweetly. She placed the chain around Mercy's neck and latched the fastener. "There."

"You look like a true princess," Henry said.

Mercy couldn't keep herself from blushing. *A gift from the general!*

After dinner, they sat near the fire together as Henry read the story of Jesus' birth from the Bible. They sang carols, ate ginger snaps, drank cider, and got their stockings full of nuts and candies. Henry danced with Mercy and Abigail as they sang and laughed.

It was a Christmas Mercy would never forget.

Chapter 20

Christmas morning had the Youngs up early. There were many preparations to complete before lunch guests began arriving. Mercy loved helping Abigail turn the tavern into a festive oasis for the soldiers and townsfolk who didn't have anywhere else to go or anyone to spend the holidays with. It brought a special kind of warmth to her heart to see the smiling faces and hear the laughter of the many men who were so far from home.

Mercy baked more ginger snaps, sugar cookies, sweet rolls, and cornbread with Abigail's supervision. David and Abe were busy kneading dough for Abigail, and they giggled continuously as the dough squished between their fingers. Henry and Benjamin were out trying their luck at finding a turkey. Abigail said it was just an excuse to get out of helping in the kitchen.

Around mid-morning, Mr. Hadley stopped by to lend a hand. Washington had given the army the day off, except for those unfortunate enough to be at their sentry posts. Abigail sent Abe to the well for some water to make tea. Abe was only gone for a moment when he came flying back through the door.

"I saw turkeys!" he said. "At the edge of the woods near the ravine."

Mr. Hadley and Mercy followed him back outside where he pointed, "Look right there, you can see four or five of 'em."

Sure enough, at the edge of the woods, strutting through the grass, were four large black specs.

"Turkeys indeed, lad!" said Mr. Hadley. "Should we try our luck?"

"We must," cried Abe. "What if Henry and Benjamin don't find any?"

Mr. Hadley fetched his musket from the tavern and loaded it with shot. He waited until the birds had disappeared over the edge of the hill and said, "Let's go."

They raced across the green and through the fields. Mercy's lungs burned as they fought for air, but she knew she had to keep up. Mr. Hadley led them to the crest of the hill ahead of where the turkeys were last seen.

Patting Abe on the shoulder, he said, "Shall we?"

Together, they crawled on their bellies towards the lip of the ravine. Mercy held her breath as they crept ever closer. When they reached the edge, Mr. Hadley slowly pointed and whispered something to Abe. Mercy watched the old man slide his musket carefully over to Abe's shoulder and then whisper again, cocking back the hammer. They waited several minutes, motionless. Then, Abe began to slowly move the muzzle of the musket, his eye fixed down the barrel.

Mercy held her hand to her chest in a futile attempt to quiet her pulse. She couldn't see anything past the two of them, but she knew the turkeys must be right there. Suddenly, Mr. Hadley made a kissing sound. Abe steadied the musket, then BOOM! Abe's little frame jerked as the musket went off. A white cloud of smoke filled the air. It took a moment for the air to clear before Mr. Hadley jumped up.

"You got 'im, lad!" He slapped Abe's back in excitement.

Abe turned to Mercy, grinning ear to ear, "I got one, Mercy!"

Mercy joined them at the lip, and together, they slid down the ravine to collect Abe's prize. It was a beautiful, and at the same time, hideous, bird. Its head was a blueish color with hints of red that resembled entrails with eyes and a beak. From its chest hung a black lock of hair about eight inches long, and from its legs protruded inch-and-a-half-long spurs.

Mr. Hadley picked up the bird and handed it to Abe. "You shoot it, you carry it!" he said with a smile.

Abe hefted the mammoth creature over his shoulder, and they climbed out of the ravine. By the time they reached the top, Abe was already exhausted and pleading with Mercy to help him carry it. Mercy found it nearly impossible to resist Abe's well-mastered "puppy face" and consented to carry the bird for a while. As she took hold, its weight surprised her—it was heavy, probably near twenty pounds.

When they were nearly to the tavern, Mercy returned the bird to Abe. "Go show Mrs. Abigail."

"Ohhh," Abe groaned. "Can you help me get it on the other shoulder? This one's bruised, for sure."

Mercy went and fetched Abigail from the kitchen.

"I heard your shot!" she said to Mr. Hadley.

"It wasn't mine, ma'am. Your lad shot the bird all on his own," Mr. Hadley said with a smile.

"We crawled to the edge of the ravine and Mr. Hadley handed me his musket and told me how to shoot it. We waited until the turkeys worked their way right in front of us. Mr. Hadley made a sound like a mouse and the turkey stopped and looked right at us! I was shakin' so bad, I just pointed in the right direction and pulled the trigger. There was so much white smoke I couldn't see a dern thing. When it cleared, there he was, floppin' at the bottom of the ravine!" Abe finished his story proudly.

"Well, looks like we won't be starving even if the men do abandon us," Abigail said, resting her hand on his shoulder proudly.

"Owww," groaned Abe. "It's a little sore."

Mr. Hadley burst out laughing and slapped him on the back, nearly knocking him over. "That's the good pain of success, lad. You're a hunter now!"

Mr. Hadley took the turkey and said, "We'll get it prepared for cookin', ma'am. Come on, lad, the work's not over yet."

Abigail smiled at Mercy and shook her head as they walked away. "God is good," she said.

It was about an hour later when the wagon pulled into the yard. Mercy and Abigail hurried out the back door, not wanting to miss the banter between hunting parties.

"Get anything?" asked Mercy.

"Not much," Henry replied, holding up a lone rabbit. "Benjamin took a shot at a couple of turkeys, but they were spooked and never stopped moving."

"Sorry," said Benjamin. "We failed to get you your Christmas turkey, ma'am."

"Oh, that's alright. I already have one," said Abigail coyly.

"You already have one?" repeated Henry, puzzled.

"Yes sir, it's right over there getting plucked for dinner." She pointed to where Abe and Mr. Hadley sat, surrounded by feathers. "Abe fetched it for me."

"Abe?" said Benjamin, his voice cracking in surprise.

"That's right, turns out he's quite the shot. Mr. Hadley lent him his musket," she said in a lofty voice.

"Abraham shot a musket?" asked Henry, dumbfounded.

"And he's got the bruise to prove it," added Mercy.

Henry and Benjamin looked at each other in shock.

"So, the next time you boys feel like abandoning us to the work while you go gallivanting around the countryside, remember this. The Lord rewards the diligent." Abigail spun around and headed back into the tavern.

Mercy watched with pleasure as the two of them fought to sort the whole thing out in their brains.

At last, it was time for Christmas night. The tavern was filled to standing room only, packed with officers and a few of the single ladies from town. Abigail played the piano, and everyone sang along. The atmosphere was warm and filled with the smells of cinnamon, cider, and the soft note of pipe tobacco.

As the people sang and danced, Mercy couldn't help but feel a sense of pride. These were free men and free women. The outcome of the war was far from certain, but they had chosen to live in this moment, free. There was no king, no regulars, no one to tell them how to live their lives. They were beholden to God, the bond of brotherhood, and a dream called liberty.

What a thing it was to behold, liberty, how few folks throughout the ages had known its taste. How blessed was she to be amongst so many who valued freedom to live more than life itself? *They deserve this night.* She thought to herself.

"Mercy?" Henry's voice brought her back. He was standing in front of her, a slight grin on his face, his upturned hand extended. "May I have the pleasure of this dance?"

Mercy nodded with a smile and took his hand. She had danced with Papa a time or two at celebrations in Lexington, so she knew enough to follow Henry's lead. The floor was filled with couples, and an officer on a violin had joined Abigail at the piano. The folks not taking part in the dance stood all around the open floor, chatting together merrily as they sipped their cider.

As the music started, Mercy felt herself move, almost as if in a dream. The couples swayed and twirled with the music; Mercy felt like a princess attending a royal ball. The only word she could think of to describe it was perfect. The whole scene was perfect.

Later that night, when all the guests had left, Henry carried sleeping Abraham and David up to bed. They had worked hard and partied even harder. Benjamin drug himself up the stairs and fell asleep the moment his head hit the pillow, judging by the almost instant snores.

Though her feet were sore, Mercy danced her way to bed. The night had been far too exciting, so she fought sleep until she etched every facet of the evening into her diary.

Chapter 21

January 25, 1776

There has been a mighty stir at the military camp today. Col. Knox arrived with a whole train of cannons from Fort Ticonderoga for the Continentals. Benjamin heard Col. Knox and his men had covered three hundred miles in the harsh cold getting them to Cambridge. Henry was asked to help move the cannons with the team. He said there are over fifty of them. The soldiers seem sure that, with these cannons, they can finally force the redcoats out of Boston.

Benjamin said he doesn't know if the redcoats being defeated in Boston would mean surrender and the end of the war, or if they would board their ships and head elsewhere in the colonies. Surrender seems the only way to get Papa back now. There have been a few prisoner exchanges over the past few months, but never for Papa. He wasn't a Continental when the war broke out, and the exchanges are usually for officers at any rate.

With so many new guns, the air is sure to be filled with thundering. The boys have taken a liking to the deafening concussion that rattles the windowpanes. I cannot imagine the sound those poor men must endure who are unfortunate enough to have to use such a weapon. I cannot bring myself to want to imagine the boys on the receiving end. Lord, please bring this conflict to a swift and just end.

Mercy Young, 13 years old.

The town was abuzz with the news of the cannons, and the new optimism put a spring in people's step and a confidence in their speech. Mercy had been sent on an errand to the general store and was trying to make her way back, but the gossip taking place here and there kept catching her by the ear and holding her back. The stalemate with the redcoats had gone on for so long that confidence in the cause had eroded considerably. It was refreshing to hear so much hope again.

Henry would be gone for most of the day again, as General Washington required the help of the team to move his new artillery. Mercy wished she could have gone along—the work seemed much more interesting than her own. Alas, she was needed at the tavern, and Abigail would be expecting her back by now.

She was in sight of the tavern when something caught her eye. A grey mass, slightly larger than a rabbit, flopped helplessly near the hedge at the edge of the yard. Walking over to investigate, Mercy saw that a young great horned owl had gotten itself tangled in a rabbit snare. In fact, the rabbit was still in the snare.

"So, you thought you'd help yourself to an easy meal, huh?" she said to the owl.

Upon hearing her voice, the owl quit fighting the snare and stared at her. Its large yellow eyes seemed to look right through her. It blinked as she approached, but didn't struggle.

Mercy carefully looked the situation over. The owl lay on its back, its feet were incredibly tangled in the fine wire, and on its legs were several lacerations where the wire had dug in. One of its wings was folded neatly along its body, while the other seemed to hang at an odd angle, as if injured.

There were a couple of obvious problems. First, the owl's feet were equipped with two-inch talons that came to a razor-sharp point. The other problem was that beak. It looked equally fearsome, with a sharp hook that ended in a point.

"If I'm gonna help you, you've got to promise not to stick me with those things," she said, trying to reason with the bird.

The owl blinked slowly as she finished, which Mercy decided to take as its agreement to her proposal. She carefully inched closer to the owl, which remained incredibly calm. It didn't seem to matter which side she approached from; the owl's head just followed her. Seeing there wasn't a blind side to this peculiar creature, she was left with no choice but to just go for it.

"Now, hold still."

Mercy reached out a trembling hand and grabbed the wire with her fingertips. She looked at the owl and the owl looked at her. Cautiously, she unwrapped one of the owl's toes—the owl just looked at her. She unwrapped another, and another, and the owl still just looked at her. Finally, one foot was free. Mercy gasped for air. She hadn't realized she was holding her breath. And the owl . . . just blinked at her.

"Okay, so far so good. You've been an excellent patient."

Again, she reached for the wire and untangled the other foot while the owl never moved—it just watched her. Once it was free, Mercy took a step back.

"Okay, you're all free," she said, but the owl didn't move. "Go on, before a cat finds you." Still, nothing.

Mercy knelt down near the owl and, reaching out, carefully tipped the bird back onto its feet. The owl hobbled a little, catching its balance, but that was it. She studied the funny bird; the one wing did appear to hang differently than the other.

"You can't fly, can you?" she said with a sigh. "Argh . . . Mrs. Abigail is going to kill me." But her mind was made up.

Mercy gently slid one hand under the bird's hurt wing and over the other. The owl didn't resist. It dawned on Mercy that it was nearly mid-morning and owls were nocturnal. The poor bird had probably been battling the snare for many hours and was exhausted. She took a deep breath and lifted the owl from the ground.

"Looks like you're coming home with me."

Mercy carried the owl right into the kitchen, where Abigail was busy baking bread for the day.

"Good heavens, Mercy, what on earth are you doing with that thing!" Abigail gasped.

"We accidentally caught it in the snare by the hedge. It was trying to steal a rabbit. I think its wing is damaged but, since it's us who made it this way, it's our responsibility to make sure it's mended . . . as one of God's creatures," she said.

Abigail studied the owl and her expression softened. "It sure is a beautiful bird. I've never laid eyes on one in my life. Look at those wise eyes."

"Will you help me fix him, Mrs. Abigail?" Mercy asked.

Abigail sighed. "Henry's gonna kill me. What seems to be wrong with it?"

"Well, besides being plum wore out, this one wing seems to hang kinda funny," Mercy answered.

Abigail eyed her. "You got a good hold on him?"

Mercy nodded. Abigail reached out and felt the wing from tip to shoulder. The owl hardly flinched.

"It doesn't seem to be broken, or even out of place, for that matter. Probably stressed it with all the flopping."

Abe and David came in from chores, followed by Benjamin.

"What is that!" exclaimed Abe as the three of them crowded around Mercy.

Mercy explained how the owl had been tangled in the snare, how it remained motionless the entire time, about the wing, and Abigail's assessment.

"Whoa! Does that mean we can keep him?" asked David.

"You'll have to convince Henry," Abigail said with a slight smile.

"Well, we can't just leave him out there to die," said Abe. "That wouldn't be proper."

"Alright, well, Henry won't be back for a while, and we have a lot of work to do. It won't help to convince him if the work's not done when he returns on account of the owl," Abigail said.

"So, what are we going to do with him in the meantime?" asked Benjamin.

"You could build him a cage, Ben," suggested Abe. "I'll work on your chores and mine until it's finished, that way everything will get done."

"Okay, I'll do my best," agreed Benjamin.

"Am I just supposed to hold him 'til then?" asked Mercy, a bit perplexed.

"Hey, you found him," said Abigail.

Everyone split up and went to work, leaving Mercy standing in the kitchen, holding the owl. As the room cleared, the owl rotated its head completely backwards and stared at Mercy.

Giggling, Mercy shook her head. "What are we gonna call you, then?"

Mercy pondered for a moment, then said, "Theo. I like the sound of that, your name will be Theo."

It took the better part of three hours before Benjamin had built a sturdy cage for Theo using tree branches and twine. The cage was an impressive five feet tall and four feet wide by four feet long. He constructed one side of the cage as a door. There were a couple of branches crisscrossed about three feet above the floor to be used as a perch.

"What do you think?" he asked Mercy.

"It's amazing!" Mercy said.

Reaching into the cage, Mercy placed Theo on the spot where the branches crossed. Feeling the branches with his feet, Theo wrapped his talons around them and held on. Swallowing hard, Mercy let go. Theo bobbed for a moment, and then, ruffling his feathers, he settled in. Benjamin closed the door and latched it with a loop.

"Good," Mercy said, rubbing her sore shoulders. "My arms were about to fall off."

"Some potato mashing will loosen those shoulders right up!" said Abigail.

Mercy groaned and followed her to the kitchen.

When Henry returned that evening, he slumped out of the wagon. He looked tired and was filthy from head to toe. After one look, Abigail muttered to Mercy that it was not a good time to spring a new family member on him. Instead, she told Mercy to get a bath drawn up and then prepared him a plate for dinner. She and the boys managed the tavern for the night, allowing Henry to recover.

Mercy was left to care for Henry, whose hands were worn and blistered. A stark contrasting line on his forehead showed where his hat had kept the dirt from reaching the skin. Tired as he was, he still managed a smile and thank you when Mercy told him the bath was ready. After he had washed and eaten, he sat in his chair, puffing on his pipe with his eyes closed. Mercy desperately wanted to tell him about Theo, but Abigail's instructions had been clear.

"I'm glad you're home," she said.

Henry managed a smile, but his eyes remained closed. "Thank you, Mercy. It's nice to be missed."

"Will you be gone again tomorrow?"

"No. We were able to get them all moved, at least for now," he said.

"Mr. Henry? I think Abigail would want you to head for bed. You look as beat as an old dog," Mercy said.

Henry chuckled. "You're probably right, Mercy." He let out a final puff of smoke and lifted himself from his chair. "Alright, I'll take your advice. I'll see you all in the morning. Don't work too hard," he said, lifting her chin briefly with a curved finger.

"See you in the morning," Mercy repeated. *I hope you wake up in a generous mood!*

That night, after the tavern closed, Abigail and the children took some of the meat from the snared rabbit from that morning and brought it out to Theo. Benjamin stuck a small chunk of it on a pointed stick and held it out to the owl. It took a few moments, but eventually the owl opened its beak and took the meat. Abe tried next, and then David. Each time, the owl took the meat and swallowed it whole.

After Theo seemed satisfied, they returned to the tavern and went to bed, or at least tried to. Mercy was so excited and anxious about what Henry would say, her mind refused to let her rest.

Chapter 22

The following morning, the Youngs raced through their chores and were ready and waiting when Henry came in for breakfast. Abigail and Mercy dished everyone up and Henry said grace. There was an awkward silence as everyone ate their food nervously. Mercy had finally built up her courage and was about to bring up the owl when Henry beat her to it.

Clearing his throat, he said, "Who wants to explain to me why we have an owl in a cage in the barn?"

"Mercy brought it home!" David exclaimed.

Henry turned his attention to Mercy; his eyes were more curious than upset. Mercy put down her fork, preparing for her explanation. She had run through it in her mind a thousand times during her sleepless night, but at the moment, she didn't feel quite as confident as she had from the safety of her blankets.

"I was on my way home from an errand, when I saw something flopping near the hedge at the edge of the yard. When I investigated, I saw that an owl had attempted to steal a rabbit from our snare and had gotten itself tangled up in the wire. After ascertaining that it would certainly die if I left it there, I carefully untangled its feet and helped it stand upright, but it wouldn't fly. Its wing seemed to have been damaged during it fight with the wire.

"Seeing how we were responsible for its condition, I felt compelled to try and save him. I brought him to the tavern and showed Mrs. Abigail, who felt his wing and didn't sense anything out of place other than it being stressed in some way. So, Benjamin built a cage for it and we fed it some rabbit meat. We were gonna ask you if it would be okay to keep him until he's well last night, but you came home tired to the bone, and we didn't want to add to your day. We decided to save the askin' 'til this morning."

When Mercy finished, everyone stopped eating and turned to Henry, waiting for his reply. He took two more bites and chewed them contemplatively. He looked up and, seeing all the eyes fixed on him, leaned back in his chair with a smirk.

"So, you say that the four of you are responsible for the plight of the poor creature that now finds itself a prisoner in my barn?" he asked rhetorically. "And as such, you are bound by responsible duty to ensure its healthy return to nature?" He took another bite, chewing slowly. He eyed Abigail, who offered an encouraging smile. "Are you in on this?"

"I was surprised as you, but after a while, he started growing on me," she confessed.

"I appear to be outnumbered," he said at last. "But once it's mended, it goes free."

A cheer went up around the table and Henry was lauded as a hero. Even Abigail celebrated.

Over the next few days, Mercy stole away every moment she could to spend time with Theo. He was fascinating. And beautiful. Mercy would talk to him about the goings on, about Papa. She brought out her books and read to him. As he improved, they carefully took him out of the cage and set him on the door of the horse stall and read to him there. He hardly ever moved. Only shifted his weight back and forth and sometimes ruffled his feathers with an enormous shake. The boys brought him a trout or a field mouse when they could catch them.

Mercy felt torn between her desire to see Theo well, and not wanting her new friend to go. At last, the inevitable day came, and in Mercy's mind it was too soon. Theo's wing was looking good. Henry thought it best to leave him out of the cage that night and give him the chance to fly off on his own.

That night, Mercy cried silently to herself. She thought about his big wise eyes, his adorable earlike feathers, the way he bobbed his head and looked at her as she read to him. She hoped he would be happy and safe, that he would live free for the rest of his days. Finally, her emotions wore her out, and she fell asleep.

Mercy woke with the first drummer's beat. Throwing off the covers, she clambered over her brothers. She quickly threw on her dress and tromped down the stairs.

Blowing by Abigail, she called over her shoulder, "I'll be right back!" and ran out the door.

Bracing herself, Mercy ducked under the lean-to of the barn.

"Theo!" she exclaimed.

Sure enough, the plump owl shook himself and stood tall as she entered. Mercy was beside herself. "I'll bet you're looking for breakfast. Stay there, I'll be right back!"

Mercy bolted for the tavern. Blasting through the door, Mercy almost knocked over Abigail, who was holding a hot pan of eggs.

"Good gracious, child, where's the fire?" she exclaimed.

"Sorry, ma'am. Theo is still in the lean-to!" Mercy blurted.

The boys stumbled down the stairs excitedly.

"Probably just decided it was easier if you fed him than to go out and find it himself," Henry said.

"Oh, I hope so," said Mercy. "Mrs. Abigail, could you spare a bit of bacon for Theo, please?"

"I don't see why not," said Abigail sweetly, almost as excited as the children.

"That thing's gonna clean us out at this rate," argued Henry. "Where's *my* bacon?"

"Stop your fussin'. I'll bring it over as soon as it's done," Abigail chided.

Mercy ripped the bacon into bite-sized pieces as she walked back to the lean-to. She was almost there when Theo flew out from under the low roof and glided in a circle above Mercy, then landed on her shoulder. His talons sank through her coat and managed to reach her skin.

"Owww!"

Theo bobbled back and forth, maintaining his balance, looking at her with his big yellow eyes.

Henry, hearing her cry, emerged to investigate. "This won't do," he said with a smirk, gently lifting Theo from her shoulder.

Mercy held up the bacon and Theo scarfed it down ravenously.

"There is a sweetness to him, isn't there?" Henry said. He carried Theo back to the lean-to and set him back on his perch. "I've got an idea of how we can give you a little protection as long as he's around."

As she walked back to the tavern, Mercy checked her shoulder; several pinpoint specks of blood dotted her skin. More than the pain, there was an excitement rising in her. Theo had the ability to leave and had stayed, and he had chosen to land on her. Would he still be there tomorrow? She had no way of knowing, but what if he chose to stay?

During the midafternoon break, when Mercy went to read to Theo, she couldn't find her coat. She was sure she had hung it up, but the empty hook couldn't lie. It was far too cold and wet to go without one, and the break in the day was limited. Eventually, she opted to use Abigail's coat and headed out.

Mercy greeted Theo warmly as she ducked under the lean-to. She stroked him gently on the head and then hopped up on a barrel. She slipped Theo some turkey from her lunch as she read to him. Her reading was becoming such a regular thing that even Abe and David sat and listened. After all, it was too cold to do much else. The time always seemed too short, and the stories always left them in suspense when they headed back to work.

When the day ended and they sat down for dinner, Henry revealed Mercy's missing coat. He had carefully sewn two decorative strips of leather from an old saddle on each shoulder. The intricate work had been restored with oil, and each side matched the other identically.

"Wow! It's beautiful," said Mercy.

"Let's see if his talons can get through that," Henry said, holding out a pair of gloves. "It would probably be wise to use these to handle him, as long as he's around, I mean."

"You'd better be careful, that just might become the latest fashion," said Abigail.

Mercy put on the coat and did a twirl. Giving Henry a hug, she thanked him.

"I must be outside my mind for letting you kids talk me into letting you keep an owl for a pet," said Henry. "I've never heard of such a thing in my life."

"Well, you have often said that these are strange times," laughed Abigail.

Henry smiled his warm smile and took a puff on his pipe. Mercy knew in her heart God had led them to this family, sure as she was breathing. They needed each other. Before Papa had even been captured, this couple had already been prepared for them. And in that moment, as Henry smiled, she thanked God for watching over them.

Chapter 23

February 28, 1776

The weather has finally begun to warm; I've been able to go without a coat on a couple of occasions. The only remnants of snow that remain from winter are those isolated in the shady places that receive no direct sunlight. The soldiers have endured a great deal over the long winter, and I find it moving that so many remain at their posts.

Henry has been called away again today at Washington's request. It seems the general is collecting all the remaining hay and straw as a part of an upcoming plan. Benjamin heard that a large supply of powder for the cannons would be delivered to the Continentals soon. Another officer said that Washington hoped to get his guns on Dorchester Heights. Henry believes that whoever gets control of the heights will turn the tide of the siege, but it would be *difficult for the Continental guns to reach the heights on account of the British Navy in the harbor watching their every move.*

Everyone seems to know that a battle is coming. That eerie uncertainty that has proven to be the prelude to any major action has descended on the town. People speak in hushed tones, unaware they are even doing it, and fear hides behind every eye. The quiet winter has left everyone on edge. The question seems to be, who will strike first?

Benjamin and Abe seem fascinated by all things military; I know they fancy themselves soldiers. For my part, I pray as Papa prayed, that the conflict will be over before they ever need to don a uniform or march to a drum.

Theo has become accustomed to riding on my shoulder. It took a little practice, but he is now quite an accomplished rider. The folks in town, especially the children, point and squeal excitedly when they see him, though he pays them little mind. Henry believes it's on account of how spoiled he is that he won't leave, but I just think he likes my stories. Tonight, he tried to follow me into the tavern after I left him under the lean-to. Abigail had a fit and swept him out with the broom.

I hope and pray that Papa has endured the winter well. We've had no word for months and I worry that something has happened to him. I try not to think about it, only to think about it all the more. All I can do is hope to see him again and keep living to that end.

Mercy Young, 13 years old.

By the time the Youngs came down for breakfast, Henry was already gone. He and the team would be assisting the Continentals in moving and piling hay and straw along the road that led to Dorchester Heights. It seemed a funny thing and an awful waste of good hay to just pile it along the road like that, but if it was part of Washington's plan, there had to be a good reason for it.

As the day went on, Mercy could see the piles of hay reaching quite high on the side of the road that faced the harbor. Wagon after wagon unloaded hay and straw until Mercy reckoned you wouldn't be able to see the road at all from the harbor. Then it hit her. That was Washington's plan; to conceal his movements on Dorchester. If the naval ships in the harbor couldn't see the troops and guns being moved, they couldn't hit them.

Mercy marveled at the simplicity of it. Only time would tell if it would really work, but if it did ... She looked out over Boston to the heights. She had witnessed enough battle to know if Washington got artillery on those hills, not a ship in the harbor would be safe. The Continentals could finally cut off the British supply line.

"Do you think it'll work?" asked Benjamin.

His voice startled her. "I hope so," she answered.

"Me too," he said. "Come on, Mrs. Abigail is waiting for you."

Turning, Mercy followed Benjamin back to the tavern. Now that she understood why the hay was along the road, a knot formed in her stomach. This was big, what was about to happen was big. And it would mean big changes. She didn't know what form those changes would take, but if this plan succeeded, for better or worse, things would not be the same.

The hay next to the road wasn't the only oddity. That afternoon and evening, the tavern was, for the most part, empty. A few townsfolk came and went, but no soldiers or even officers. It was strangely quiet. And there it was again, that eerie calm before the storm.

When Henry returned shortly after dark, he confirmed her suspicions. He didn't know when, but soon Washington was going to move on Dorchester. Not only that, but Washington had requested the help of the tavern to keep the troops fed and watered while they work.

"An officer will contact us when it's time," said Henry.

"Will we be in danger?" asked Abigail.

"I don't believe so. We'll probably use the wagon to ferry supplies to the garrison at Roxbury and care for the soldiers there."

Roxbury was a smaller town than Cambridge, nearly halfway between the tavern and the heights. Due to its proximity to the harbor, the garrison had taken a terrible beating from the naval ships over the months since the war began.

Abigail looked at Henry uneasily.

"The soldiers will all be working night and day," said Henry. "We will be blessed to do them this small service."

"And what of the tavern?" she asked.

"I don't think there will be many folks not involved with this plan. We can close up for a day or two if need be." Henry put his arm around her and pulled her close. "We'll get through this."

Chapter 24

March 2 started with a bang, or more of a boom. Cannons set the tavern to trembling at dawn, nearly shaking the Youngs out of bed. Mercy and the boys flew to the window. The haze of cannon smoke rose from Roxbury, Cambridge and Prospect Hill. The Continentals were bombarding the British positions in Boston.

Mercy had never witnessed so many cannons firing at once; it was awesome and terrible. Down below, in Boston, she could see redcoats scurrying about as earth and buildings erupted around them. She couldn't imagine the fear of feeling so trapped with such a fury bearing down on you. Cannon after cannon shook the tavern. After so many months of quiet, she regretted wishing for this day.

There was a knock at the door, and Henry stepped in.

"It's begun," he said. "We need to get through chores quickly and load the wagon with provisions and water. The soldiers are going to start working towards Dorchester Heights."

The Youngs plowed through their chores and met Henry at the back of the tavern. The wagon was already harnessed to the team, and several empty barrels lined the sides.

"We are going to form a line between the well and each barrel and pass these pails person to person until they are all full, understand?" Henry asked. Everyone nodded.

Henry manned the well while the others passed the buckets. It was hard work, and Mercy wished she had put on the leather gloves that Henry had given her. It took nearly an hour to fill all the barrels. Mercy's hands were blistered, and she wasn't the only one. The day was cool, but even so, sweat ran down her neck.

"Good work, everyone," Henry said, wiping his forehead with the back of his hand. "Get some water yourselves and we'll take a little break before moving on."

The bombardment had eased a bit, though there was rarely a minute without a cannon going off somewhere.

Mercy dipped the ladle into the water pail and was bringing it to her mouth when the navy cut loose with all its cannons on Roxbury and the fortifications below Cambridge. The ladle involuntarily jumped from her hand and they all dove behind the wagon.

"Seems like the redcoats have had enough of that," Henry said, lifting David off the ground and dusting him off. "Their guns can't reach us up here, not without putting their ships at risk."

The Continentals unleashed their own response on Boston and the buildings at the edge of town paid for it dearly. The constant vibration of the ground, coupled with this stench of sulfur, was nauseating. It was a never-ending tremor that ripped through the entire body, making you feel uneasy everywhere. Even the horses pawed and shifted in their traces, and Theo had left Mercy's shoulder for the lean-to.

An officer on a chestnut horse rode up to the wagon. He sat tall and unflinching in the saddle. "The boys will be starting their work on Dorchester; we'll need your support as soon as you can afford it."

Henry nodded his understanding.

"Godspeed!" the officer shouted and galloped off.

Henry looked over his exhausted crew. "This is going to be a long day, so take care of yourselves. But we are fortunate to be here for a time such as this, if this is our part, then let us do it well. I have a feeling, when it's all said and done, these events will go down in the history books. You'll be able to tell your children and their children that you were here."

Henry looked at them all affectionately. "Right, well, we'll divide into two teams. Benjamin and David, you will stay here and help Abigail prepare what she needs and be ready to help refill the barrels when we return from Roxbury. I'll take Mercy and Abe to help distribute water and rations, and care for any wounds we may encounter."

"Why aren't I coming with you?" asked Benjamin. "I'm brave and strong."

"That's exactly why I need you here. I need someone brave and strong to help and watch over Abigail and David while I'm away. I need a man at both ends of this endeavor, and you are that man," Henry said, holding out his hand.

Benjamin took it, and Henry gave him a firm handshake. "I'm counting on you."

Mercy and Abe collected several dippers and climbed into the wagon. As they pulled away, David ran after them, waving and hollering, "Be careful!"

Bumping along the road, Mercy couldn't tell if she was shaking, or it was just the wagon. Her body had not forgotten its last taste of combat, and it was in no hurry to get another.

The cannon fire and explosions grew more distinct as they approached Roxbury. Columns of soldiers, now hidden from the redcoats by the piles of hay, carried shovels, picks, and axes. They looked more like miners than soldiers. There must have been thousands of them, like ants, clearing a path up the heights, concealed by hay and cannon fire.

Henry pulled up behind a battered but still standing building and climbed into the back of the wagon with Abe and Mercy. As the units of soldiers working on the hill were replaced by fresh units, they filed by the wagon for bread and water.

Mercy watched them as they sat with their backs against the wall. The soldiers were covered with dirt, sweat left trails on their faces, their hands were filthy as they wolfed down the bread. The soldiers did not laugh, or joke, or even smile like Mercy was so accustomed to in the tavern. They looked afraid and tired; they looked like ordinary people.

When the navy unleashed another volley on Roxbury, everyone got low and covered their heads. But the fortifications were strong, and the cannonballs had little effect unless, by chance, it scored a direct hit.

It was a good two hours before the wagon ran dry. Mercy, Abe, and Henry had served a couple hundred soldiers, at least. Washington's cannons had continued to bombard Boston, and the British had continued to respond.

Their return trip included dropping off two wounded Continentals at the doctor. The men had been unfortunate enough to be on the receiving end of a mortar round. Their bodies had been peppered with bits of shrapnel; it was unlikely either one would survive.

She didn't know what compelled her, but as they rode, she climbed in the back, and squatting between them, held their hands. One of the soldiers had already slipped into unconsciousness while the other moaned and whimpered as the wagon bounced down the road.

Mercy watched a tear chase its way down the man's cheek, then, he was gone. "I'm sorry," Mercy said, placing his hand on his chest.

She looked out the back of the wagon and shook her head. It was pitiful, dying this way. History wouldn't remember these two men. Their families, if they had any, wouldn't find out for weeks they were gone. All for a cause that was still so uncertain, for a hope and a dream that had never been tested. How much more pitiful, though, she thought, would it be to live your life without ever finding a cause or a hope worth dying for? Perhaps these men, though they died young, had lived richer lives *because* of purpose than the many who live long and never find it.

Looking back at the two men, she decided that she would remember them if no one else did. She didn't know their names, but she would write about them in her diary, and some day, she would share the story of their bravery and sacrifice with her children. In that way, they wouldn't be forgotten.

When the wagon pulled in at the doctor's, Henry jumped down to fetch the help, but Mercy caught him by the arm and shook her head. Henry looked into the wagon and his shoulders slumped.

"They've been gone for a little while now," Mercy said softly.

"We'll drop them at the army camp; the grave detail will take care of them from there," Henry said.

He climbed back into the wagon and snapped the reins. At the army garrison, one of the few soldiers left on duty directed them to a small tent on the northern edge. Henry, with the help of a soldier, placed the bodies in the tent, then they started for home. The day was only half over, and Mercy was already too exhausted for words.

At the tavern, they took a short rest as the others reloaded the wagon with bread and water. Abigail looked tired; the constant bombardment was wearing her down.

"Can't we have a moment's peace?" she groaned.

"Unfortunately, it looks as though it will be the same tomorrow. The work on the Heights is going ahead slowly; it's going to take another day," Henry replied.

Abigail took a determined breath and said, "What am I complaining about, it's not me those guns are shooting at."

Henry kissed her tenderly on the head. "Come along then, let's get that wagon filled up."

Once again, they loaded the barrels, everyone waved their goodbye, and they were off for Roxbury. They didn't make it more than a hundred yards from the tavern when a familiar friend landed on the lip of a barrel next to Mercy.

"Theo!" she exclaimed.

It was his first time flying so far since his injury. He eyed her expectantly as if to say "Where's my lunch?" Mercy stroked him on the head.

"What are you doing so far from home? Are you going to help with the water as well?" she asked.

Theo bobbed his head excitedly, which made Mercy laugh.

"Here," said Henry, handing her a piece of jerky. "Soften this up and he can have it."

"I knew you liked him," Mercy said triumphantly, taking the jerky.

Henry turned his head, pretending he didn't hear her. Mercy bit off a bit of the jerky and chewed it some before offering it to Theo. He took it and gulped it down ravenously and then he bobbed his head again.

"How did you ever manage to survive without me?" she teased, handing him another piece.

Mercy felt a bit of gloom lift from the day with the presence of her friend. The cannon fire didn't seem to bother Theo, and his courage helped feed her own. Theo seemed to work wonders on the soldiers from the Heights as well. They smiled and laughed while talking about Theo and Mercy as they drank their water and ate bread. His curious nature had a way of helping everyone forget the horror of the circumstance they were all in.

As each new unit came to the wagon, Theo would charm them. One man, who heard Theo was there, brought him a field mouse he scared up while working. The man tossed the mouse in the air towards the wagon. As soon as Theo saw it, he blasted off into the air and caught the mouse before it hit the ground. He circled the wagon once and landed next to Mercy with his prize. A cheer went up from all the soldiers who witnessed it. Mercy tried to play it cool, but inside, she was dumbfounded.

"Good boy, Theo," she said, stroking his head. Theo just blinked once and then swallowed the mouse whole.

As the day wore on, several more mice showed up, and several more feats of aerial acrobatics were conducted. At some point, Theo became full because, instead of eating the last few mice, he offered them to Mercy. Not knowing what to do, Mercy pet him on the head and placed the mice in her apron pocket. This seemed to convince Theo she had eaten them.

The day was growing dark, and the officer on the chestnut horse asked their assistance again for the next day. On their ride home, all they could talk about was Theo. Even Henry agreed he was like medicine to the troops working on the heights.

When they were in sight of the lantern hanging from the tavern, the cannon fire ceased. The silence that followed was more deafening than the noise before. Mercy heard everything as if it were the first time; the leftover water sloshing in the barrels, the squeak of the buckboard, the crushing of gravel under the wagon wheels, even Theo's soft cooing. It was all so loud.

Henry noticed it too and called the horses to a stop. They sat in the silence for a moment.

"That's incredible," said Abe. "I think I can hear my own heartbeat."

Mercy thought it unsettling that one could grow so accustomed to that merciless racket that silence would cause you to recoil. To grow so accustomed to war that peace was able to offend. It had only taken a day and her ears, at least, had accepted it as normal.

That night, everyone climbed into bed exhausted and slept like rocks.

Chapter 25

The thunder of dozens of cannons and mortars going off all at once drove the Youngs from their sleep for the second day in a row. There was a universal groan that went up as young bodies stretched sore muscles. No one went to the window, no one looked towards Boston, no one dove to the floor when the navy returned fire. Everyone knew the redcoats couldn't reach the tavern.

At the bottom of the stairs, Mercy saw that it wasn't Abigail, but Henry working breakfast. Abigail sat at the table sipping a cup of tea; the night had not done her any favors. She looked tired, and somehow older. Her bright cheery smile was replaced with a grim expression, and her bright eyes seemed distant now. When she saw the Youngs, the smile she offered was forced.

"Whoa, Mrs. Abigail, you look rough," said Abe.

Mercy clapped her hand over his mouth. "Abraham Young!" Mercy started.

"It's okay, Mercy," said Abigail. "He's just being honest. It's one of the things I admire about him, always honest." Abigail said as sweetly as she could manage. "Besides, you look rough yourself, Abe!" she said. Then she burst out laughing.

This set everyone to laughing, and with tears running down her face, Abigail opened up her arms and the Youngs gave her a warm hug.

"Thank you," Abigail said, "that was just what I needed."

With cannons echoing all around the harbor, the team loaded the wagon with water and bread. Theo watched them curiously from atop the tavern peak. As Mercy, with aching muscles, lifted another pail of water into the wagon, she shook her head. *He really was a spoiled owl.* When it came time for them to start off for Roxbury, Mercy called to him. Theo took a hop and then effortlessly glided down to the wagon.

Like the day before, the din of cannon fire and explosions was exponentially more intense as they drew nearer to Roxbury. The columns of soldiers with their land clearing gear were already hard at work, clearing the way up Dorchester Heights.

As Mercy had predicted, the number of dead mice that came flying towards the wagon had multiplied immensely. Theo stayed busy with a constant acrobatic display as he caught them in his sharp talons. By the end of their first run, Mercy's pocket was near to bursting with mice. The thought of it disgusted her, but she didn't have the heart to disappoint Theo, who had such great pleasure in delivering them to her.

On their way back to the tavern, a stray cannonball exploded near the road, setting the stack of hay on fire. Henry pulled the wagon to a stop and handed pails to a unit of soldiers frantically trying to beat the flames out. Together, they used the icy water from the ditches to subdue the flames. When Henry returned to the wagon, he was wet clear up above the knee, panting, and his face was marked with soot.

"I think it's out now," he said, handing Mercy and Abe the pails. "That was a little too close for comfort."

In a moment, the team was pulling for home again. Mercy slid herself to the edge of the buckboard and, keeping an eye on Theo, she began dumping her cache of mice, one at a time. Each time he turned to look at her, she would simply stroke him on the head and smile until he looked away. She counted twenty-seven when, at last, she reached the end of them.

Pulling into the yard, Mercy could hear Abigail humming a hymn over the more distant drumming of the cannons. The smell of fresh baked bread wafted through the air out of the open kitchen door. David was busy playing in a puddle which had formed from the ruts of the wagon wheels. Benjamin and Abigail emerged from the tavern to meet them.

Abigail rushed to Henry when she saw his state. "Good heavens, what happened to you?" she asked.

"Nothing serious, there was a fire on the road, and we helped put it out, that's all," Henry responded, giving her a hug. "We're alright, Abigail."

"Thank the Good Lord for that, I've been praying all morning. Come wash up, Benjamin and I have prepared lunch."

"What's it like down there?" Benjamin asked Mercy.

"Loud and dusty," replied Abe.

"Did you hear anything about the progress on the Heights?" asked Benjamin.

"An officer told Mr. Henry that they will be hauling the guns up the hill tonight, but that's only after they clear some of the trees and build fortifications in the pitch dark with nothing but moonlight to work by," Mercy answered.

"Did he sound confident?" asked Benjamin.

"He sounded like he was under orders," Mercy replied.

When they entered the tavern, Abigail and Henry were in the middle of a similar conversation.

"They're going to need us tonight," Henry said.

"With no rest? There will be nothing left of us by morning," Abigail objected.

"By morning, the guns will be on the Heights and the redcoats will have no choice but to surrender," Henry replied confidently.

"And if they don't?" asked Abigail.

"Then they will be destroyed," said Henry.

Abigail sighed. "What choice do we have? Can't let those boys drop dead from thirst when we could have done something about it."

"No, we can't," agreed Henry.

Mercy loved watching Henry and Abigail love each other. They were perfect, not because they did everything perfectly, but because they loved as perfectly as they knew how. She reckoned there weren't two people on earth who believed in each other as much as they did.

"We're all washed up, ma'am," blurted out Abe.

Abigail turned from Henry with her normal cheery smile. "Right, Benjamin and I worked up some cornbread with honey, ham, and potatoes for our hard-working family," she said as they all sat down.

"Benjamin made cornbread?" asked Abe.

"Sure did, and I helped," said David.

"We've got to keep up our strength. Henry tells me we will be at this all night," Abigail sighed.

"The Continentals are going to get those guns up on the Heights tonight, I know they will," Henry said.

"Are they going to be shooting off the cannons all night?" asked David with a groan.

"I suspect so. If the redcoats catch wind of what's happening on the Heights before the fortifications are made, they'll blast that hilltop with everything they've got. Washington's got to keep their heads down until the guns are in place," Henry replied.

"We'll all be deaf by then," Abe said.

"That reminds me," said Abigail. "Mr. Hadley said to stuff some cotton fluff in your ears. He said that's what the soldiers do. I gave it a try; it's a little funny at first, but if it weren't for the rumble, I would hardly know they were going off. I put some in a basket by the door."

"If the redcoats surrender, do we get Papa back?" David asked.

There was a long pause. Then Henry answered, "If the British surrender completely and give us our freedom, then yes, I believe both sides will exchange all their prisoners and the war will be over."

"Good," said David. "I'll keep praying that they surrender then."

"Me too," said Mercy.

After lunch, they loaded the wagon for another run to Roxbury. The incessant volley of cannon fire barely rose above the sound of her own heartbeat in Mercy's cotton-filled ears. Theo had had enough chaos for the day and remained under the lean-to, asleep.

Mercy looked out towards Boston as they rode along. Smoke rose from several buildings. The Boston neck was pocked with craters. Plumes of dirt and smoke burst into the air in and around the city as the cannon balls continuously rained down. Groups of skirmishers advanced and retreated on British positions on the neck. *All part of Washington's distraction.*

The British navy appeared to have bought the ruse as they concentrated their cannon fire on defending the neck. This would be a welcome reprieve for the men in Roxbury and those working on the Heights. Mercy wondered how many of the Continentals selling Washington's deception on the neck would give their lives so that the work could be completed on the Heights.

The soldiers in Roxbury looked tired. They had been clearing land for two days and the job wasn't over. Several cannons lined the road now, and a couple teams of oxen stood lazily nearby. Several hundred men sat concealed behind the buildings and stacks of hay, waiting for nightfall and the work remaining at the top of the hill.

They handed out food and water, and Mercy volunteered to help Officer Davis, a young medical officer, bandage wounded and blistered hands. Even in their battered state, the men's spirits were high. They seemed to know the enormous weight of their mission and were confident that they could achieve it. In every one of them, Mercy saw Papa.

"Are you the girl who kept that redcoat from skewering Hadley?" a soldier asked as she wrapped his hand.

Mercy nodded shyly.

"He's a long-time friend of mine, more like a brother, really. He's been a different man since that day. I think you saved his life in more ways than one. Thank you for that."

"You're welcome," Mercy said, finishing with the bandage.

"You're good at this," the man said.

"At what?" Mercy asked, puzzled.

"Mercy," the man replied.

As night fell, the work on Dorchester reached the crest of the heights and the sounds of felling trees and hundreds of picks and shovels would no longer be deadened by the hill. The Continental cannon fire intensified, masking the sounds traveling across the harbor. Washington's cover was further aided by the indignant return fire from Boston and the Royal Navy.

In the moonlight, the soldiers formed into ranks and marched up to the crest of Dorchester Heights.

Chapter 26

The work on the crest was desperate. If everything wasn't in place by morning, the Royal Navy would blast the crest of the hill to oblivion. Due to this fact, the officer on the chestnut horse requested Henry to drive the wagon of food and water to the crest of the hill so the soldiers wouldn't have to take the time to walk down.

The newly created road was steep, and the horses strained to get the full barrels of water up the hill; but at last, with Henry's encouragement, they accomplished the task. From the crest of the hill, Mercy could see all of Boston below. It seemed so close she thought that someone with a good arm could hit it with a rock, though common sense told her that would be impossible.

Explosions radiated flashes of light into the night as cannons fired and mortars exploded. The scene was intense and awesome. A flash of light reflected off the water as the Royal

Navy let loose a volley. The echo reverberated off the harbor like she had never heard it before. Fires burned below her in Roxbury and in Boston, torches illuminated the forward positions of both contenders on the Neck. The whole war was on full display from the crest of the hill.

All around her, men worked. They felled each tree, stripped it of its limbs, and chunked it into workable lengths. Other men threw ropes with grapples up into standing trees, while soldiers with axes chipped away at the trunks. A third group of men with shovels and picks worked on a stump that was roped to a team of oxen. Not a single torch blazed. Moonlight was the only light they worked by.

Mercy was busily handing out water to a crew that had just ended their shift when a shout rang out.

"Look out!"

A massive tree slammed to the ground, its branches thrashing the wagon. Mercy froze; the four men she was serving had disappeared in the branches. From everywhere, soldiers appeared, rifling through the branches, looking for their comrades. They pulled two from the branches, battered with cuts and bruises, but alive. A third had to be cut free by men with axes, carefully cutting away large branches. The fourth man was under a large section of trunk, alive but unconscious. It took a good while to remove the trunk, but at last, the man was free.

Mercy jumped down from the wagon and began tending to the first two men. The medical officer was beside her working on the third, while another soldier helped Henry empty the wagon of the barrels. They placed the third and fourth men in the wagon; they needed immediate medical care if they were to survive the night.

Henry jumped onto the buckboard and called out, "Mercy!"

Mercy looked at him, and then back to the injured soldiers. "I'll stay with them," she said.

Henry stared at her for a moment.

"It's alright, sir," said Officer Davis. "I'll watch out for her."

Henry hesitated a moment longer, then cracking the reins hard, yelled, "Yaw!" And the wagon tore off down the hillside.

Mercy and the medical officer worked feverishly on the other two patients. The scene was terrifying, and had she thought about where she was, about the mortars exploding midair, the workers felling trees all around her, of being alone, it would have been too much. But here, just like with Mr. Hadley, all she could see was a man, a wounded man, who needed her help.

Mercy tore a piece of fabric from the edge of her dress and dipped it in a pail of water. Dabbing at the man's wounds, she washed away the dirt and debris. When she finished with one wound, the medical officer bandaged it and she moved on to clean another wound. The man's elbow was clearly shattered, and Mercy dabbed it as delicately as she could. The soldier moaned as she worked.

Officer Davis leaned over and whispered loudly in her ear. "Don't waste too much time on that, he won't keep it." His tone was remorseful, but sure.

Swallowing down the lump in her throat, she moved to the second man. When they finished, the medical officer handed her a ladle of water.

"This is only the beginning," he said somberly. "They'll be working like this all night."

After Mercy took a drink, she handed the ladle back.

"You mean a lot to these men," he said, pointing around. "Your courage gives them strength."

Mercy gave him a sheepish smile.

"Get a little rest, they'll be needing our help again soon."

Mercy sat back against one of the barrels, her hands shaking. She wished Theo were there; his curious sweet face always brought her peace. At this moment, she found herself in the midst of a storm like none she had ever known. She drank another ladle of water and closed her eyes.

Officer Davis wasn't wrong; it had only been thirty minutes since the last accident when a grappling hook sprung free, catching a man in the chest. Two soldiers carried him over and placed him beside the other two, waiting for Henry to return. The medical officer cut the man's shirt off and instructed Mercy to clean the area around the hook. The man groaned in pain, and the officer fought to keep him from grabbing the hook as Mercy worked.

At last, Henry returned with the wagon and the three men were wedged on board. Mercy knew he wanted to check on her, but they were needed where they were. Another crack of the reins set the wagon in motion, and Henry disappeared over the hill again.

Mercy and Officer Davis worked far into the night. Henry returned time and time again to drop off bread and water and bring back injured men. The work progressed slowly as each tree had to be felled, limbed, chunked, and the stump removed. The men labored long and hard. More than a dozen fell out on account of exhaustion.

At last, the trees had been cleared, and the fortifications were complete. All that remained was to move the cannons from the base of the hill into position. They harnessed the oxen, and the first cannon began to make its way up the road. Several soldiers leaned hard on the wheels to help them roll as the oxen pulled. The road was slick with mud from the night's work, and the oxen fought for footing.

When the cannon was three-quarters of the way up the hill, one of the oxen slipped, landing on its front knees. The cannon lurched backwards, and the soldiers fought to hold it. The ox slipped again as it staggered to its feet and the wheels rolled over a soldier on either side. The soldiers pulled the crushed men out of the way, but there was no time to stop. They needed the momentum to get the cannon up the hill.

The injured soldiers were moved to the side of the road and left for Mercy and the medical officer to work on in the mud. Mercy slid down the hillside, past the cannon with a pail of water. She cradled the first soldier's head in her lap and gave him some water to drink. The medical officer cut away the man's trousers to assess the damage. His thigh was clearly broken, but apart from the break, there were no open wounds.

They moved to the second man. His foot was crushed, and his head had a severe gash. Mercy tore another rag from her dress and dipped it in the water. She hummed one of Abigail's hymns as she rinsed the wound. Officer Davis reached into his satchel for a dressing but came up empty. Smiling wryly at the pitiful situation, Mercy held up the edge of her apron; it was the only remotely clean cloth left. The exhausted officer nodded his thanks and cut out a bandage with his scissors.

There wasn't an inch of either of them that wasn't covered with mud, sweat, and blood. Mercy washed her hands in the pail of water and splashed her face. She was exhausted, beyond exhausted, she felt nothing. The ache in her muscles was replaced by a numb tingling; the world moved in slow motion around her and her thoughts all ran together.

"Think we can get them to the bottom of the hill?" Officer Davis asked.

Mercy stared through him blankly.

"Mercy!" he shouted.

Her eyes focused on his.

"Can you help me get them to the bottom of the hill? The wagon can't get to them here with all the cannons on the road," he said again.

Mercy nodded slowly, and the medical officer staggered his way up the hill to fetch the gurney.

When he returned, they carefully placed the first man on the gurney. Mercy took the feet end, and the officer led the way at the front. Mercy strained to lift the man; her muscles had nothing left to give. She willed herself to stand and, with grit teeth, Mercy lifted the stretcher from the ground. Painstakingly, they worked and slipped their way down the hill, past the second team of oxen with another cannon, all the way to the bottom.

Setting the man gently on the ground, the officer turned to Mercy. "I feel ashamed to ask, but there's no one else to help. Will you help me carry just one more?"

Without responding, Mercy turned and started back up the hill. After loading the second man, they started down the hill once more. Mercy fell to her knees multiple times, crawling the gurney forward. As they reached the bottom of the hill, Henry was just pulling in. The faint grey of predawn was just beginning to glow in the east.

Seeing Mercy, Henry jumped out of the wagon and took her end of the gurney. Mercy stumbled forward as the weight was lifted. She managed one more step, her head spun, the din of cannon fire grew distant, and her world went black.

The last thing she heard was Henry's voice yelling, "Mercy! Mercy!"

Chapter 27

When Mercy awoke, the room was bright with sunlight. The song of birds in the trees outside the window mixed with the dull thud of an axe splitting wood. At first, the sounds alarmed her. *Where was the bombardment?*

Looking towards the window, she saw Henry sleeping uncomfortably in a chair beside the bed, a crocheted blanket draped over his shoulders. She looked herself over. She was clean from top to bottom, and in new undergarments. Her hands were wrapped in several places and were stiff and sore to move. Sitting up, she realized she was stiff and sore everywhere. There was a dull ache in her head, but it was no longer pounding. She couldn't remember how she'd gotten there, but she did remember the night on the hill.

The small clock on the wall read ten-thirty. Since there didn't seem to be any hurry, Mercy decided to listen to the tingling in her muscles and enjoy the rest. David's laughter in the yard brought a smile to her face, and the day itself seemed to have a weight lifted. Beside her, Henry shifted in his sleep and the blanket slid from his shoulders. Mercy leaned over and put it back in its place.

"Oww," she whispered. She was REALLY sore.

Footsteps on the stairs refocused her attention on the door. The handle turned and Abigail walked in carrying a serving tray with a teapot and cups. When her eyes met Mercy's, she began to tremble. Setting the tray on the nightstand, she walked over to the bed and sat down.

"Bless the Lord," she said as tears rolled down her cheeks. "Bless the merciful Lord."

She cupped Mercy's face in her hands and kissed her on the forehead. "How many times am I going to almost lose you, my treasured child?"

Henry stirred beside the bed.

"He hasn't left your side since he brought you home," Abigail said. "Not for a moment."

"How long have I been asleep?"

"A day and a half," answered Abigail. "I've never seen anyone so exhausted in all my life. I bathed you; I dressed you, and still, you wouldn't wake up." She wiped a tear from her cheek. "You were so filthy I didn't even recognize you at first."

She smiled sadly. "I had to burn your dress, or what was left of it."

Abigail took a deep breath. "That young medical officer stopped by three times to check on you. I reckon he'll be by again before day's end. He said those boys would have died without you. He felt so bad about your dress, he left some money so I could fetch you a new one," she chuckled.

"Why has the bombardment stopped?" Mercy asked.

"That's right, you wouldn't know about that, would you?" Abigail clasped Mercy's hands. "We won, child! The British have surrendered Boston! The Continentals never even fired the guns on the Heights; just seein' them up there was enough. They're busy pulling out as we speak. General Washington made a deal with the British general that if the redcoats spared the town, they could leave in peace."

"And Papa?"

"No one's heard yet what will become of the prisoners, but we're all praying."

The chair beside the bed creaked and Henry sat up. "Mercy," he said with a smile. "How are you?"

"I'm fine, Mr. Henry, just a little sore in some places."

"That makes two of us," he said. "You gave us quite a scare. I turned around from setting down that gurney and you were lying in the mud."

"I'm sorry. Mrs. Abigail said I was a bit of a mess."

"That's an understatement," said Henry.

Mercy blushed.

"It's nice hearing the birds again," Mercy said, changing the subject.

"Aye, it is," replied Henry.

"Well, when you feel up to it, I'll fetch you some breakfast. There's no hurry; we'll take care of the tavern 'til you recover your strength," said Abigail.

Throughout the day, many visitors stopped by to check on Mercy. The boys took their turn and told her all about how Theo was doing, about the British surrendering, and what a mess she was when Henry brought her home. Next was Mr. Hadley, who chided Mercy for her reckless behavior, asking what good it was to save his life only to kill him by giving him a heart attack. He gave her a bag of candy he'd snuck past Abigail.

After Mr. Hadley, the medical officer stopped by. He treated Mercy like a patient, checking her vitals, and prescribing care. He updated her on the men they had treated together; they hadn't lost a single one. He said the men had asked for her, and that when she was able, it would do them all good if she came by the medical tent to see them. The one soldier had indeed lost his arm, and one of the men crushed by the cannon had lost his foot. But they had survived.

"I was so exhausted that night," confessed Officer Davis. "But I couldn't quit because you wouldn't quit. Every part of me wanted to. If you hadn't trudged back up that hill, I don't believe I would have been able to compel myself to. You saved those men, Mercy. And I hoped you would recover so I could tell you that." The officer squeezed Mercy's hand, tipped his hat to Henry, and walked out the door.

Mercy didn't know what to feel. She hadn't thought about what she was doing; she simply saw something that needed doing and did it. She didn't believe anyone would have done less.

Mercy watched a tear roll down Henry's cheek. "Oh, stop makin' a fuss," she said with a smile. "Everyone is alright now."

Henry nodded his head in agreement and wiped the tear away. "You're right, it's too pretty a day for tears." Standing up, he offered her his hand. "You ready to head downstairs?"

Mercy got up and put on the new dress Abigail had bought for her. Brushing her hair took effort, but she managed it. She met Henry outside the door, and taking his hand, made her way down the stairs. To her surprise, Theo sat on a constructed perch near the bottom of the stairs. He bobbed his head excitedly when he saw her.

"When did he . . .?"

"It was a moment of weakness," Henry said, clearing his throat.

She stroked the soft feathers of his head. "Did you miss me?"

"He eats better than I do," Henry complained.

Putting on the leather gloves, she called to Theo. He hopped off the perch and glided to her hand. Together, they walked out into the bright sunlight. It felt good to have the sun on her face, a light breeze tickling the skin on her neck.

The boys were busy playing war in the yard. It looked like Benjamin had taken David prisoner and Abe was working hard to get him back. Mercy closed her eyes and took it all in. *Peace.* It was the first time in over a year she had known peace.

Mercy looked out over Boston, smoke still rose from ramparts and dilapidated buildings. Ships at the dock were busy with activity, the British garrisons were sparsely manned. It seemed funny how different one day could be from the next, from peace to war to peace again.

Abe collapsed on the ground beside her. "I'm hit! Save me, Mercy."

Mercy shook her head and laughed. "I'm not quite ready for that again yet."

Abe rolled to his feet and took off for the bushes with his branch musket.

"You'd think they'd be ready to play 'peace' after what we've just been through," Abigail complained.

"They're just preparing for the next war," Mercy lamented.

That night, they sat around a fire in the ring. Henry puffed on his pipe while Abigail knitted. Theo sat on Mercy's shoulder.

Abigail tried to protest, saying she was in no condition to have anything on her shoulders just yet, but Mercy insisted it was where he belonged. Mr. Hadley joined them after a bit and, with his harmonica, he entertained them all with lively tunes. Spring was in the air, and new beginnings with it.

Chapter 28

March 16, 1776

I visited the medical tent today. It was good to see smiles on so many faces. I felt a little embarrassed as the men cheered my arrival. Many of them won't be able to return to service on account of their injuries. I only hope they can have some form of a decent life as payment for the sacrifices they have made. Theo behaved himself well enough, even accepting food from their hands. He never fails to bring a smile to the faces of the people we meet. He's become quite picky on account of all the pampering he receives.

Henry said that the last of the British will be pulling out of Boston in the next couple of days. Still no word on Papa, though Mr. Hadley said that General Washington was working towards a full prisoner exchange. I pray his time on the ship has not changed him, though I am sure I've changed.

Officer Davis stopped by today. I told him about the dull headaches that have constantly plagued me since the night of the third. His only consolation was that he gets them too, and that he hopes by God's grace they will pass in time. He has become a family friend and a dispatch carrier between the wounded soldiers and me, though he doesn't seem to mind.

Life has returned to its mundane rhythm, and for that, I am thankful. There are more than enough adventures to be had without the suffering of war being a part of it. I have made it my aim to be grateful for the little things and moments that make life so sweet, and to see the blessing even in the bad days, knowing they could be much worse.

Finally, I am thankful for my family. The road that brought us together was a difficult one, but who we have become is well worth the suffering. Even if it is only for this little while until we get Papa back, we've been blessed to call this tavern home.

Mercy Young, 13 years old.

The next morning, Abigail sent Mercy on an errand into town to purchase more thread at the general store. Abe was wearing out trousers faster than Abigail could repair them. Walking along, Mercy took in the sights and sounds. She loved going to town; the blacksmith hammered a horseshoe, soldiers marched on the green, hammers drove nails, horses clopped, and people chatted. Men tipped their hats as she passed, and Mercy nodded her acceptance. The town was alive again.

She completed her business at the store and made her way back to the tavern. As she approached, she noticed a brilliant white stallion tied to the hitching post. A second horse, a darker grey, was tied beside it and a soldier stood beside them. It was odd to see strange horses at this time in the morning, as the tavern wouldn't be open for business until noon.

Reaching the door, Mercy nodded to the soldier, who directed her with his hand inside. Entering, Mercy saw a man in a grand military uniform sitting at the long table. It was General Washington. When she entered, he stood and bowed to her.

"Are you the angel I've heard so much about?" he asked.

Mercy looked at him, puzzled.

"My soldiers have told me many stories about a young girl who threw herself on one of my men to protect him from an enemy bayonet. A girl who fooled the Tories by scolding them to shame and rescued my precious munitions. A girl who lifted their spirits with bread and water, and the antics of a peculiar little owl. A girl who tirelessly cared for them on that terrible night on Dorchester Heights when there was no one else. A girl who nearly gave her life for our cause. Are you that girl?"

His tone was gentle and sincere, not at all how Mercy had expected a general to sound. His face was warm and kind, though his eyes betrayed his regal stance, revealing exhaustion and sorrow. Mercy knew the weight of every battle, every soldier, every loss, was on his shoulders.

She nodded shyly. "Yes, sir."

The general held out his gloved hand, and Mercy placed hers in it. The general leaned over and kissed it gently.

"Thank you, Mercy," he said softly.

Standing upright, General Washington took a more serious tone. "I heard about your father, one of the brave men who took the field at Lexington. On hearing of your heroics, I endeavored to find a way to repay you for your compassion towards my men. After the British surrendered in Boston, I made every attempt to secure the release of your father, only to discover the prison ship set sail for England a week prior to our victory. Regrettably, your father is bound for London and will be imprisoned there for the duration of the war."

Mercy felt herself grow weak, and she caught the edge of the table to steady herself. She fought the urge to panic as her breathing increased rapidly.

"Oh no, Papa . . ." she breathed.

The general continued. "Upon hearing the news, I had thought it best to send a subordinate to deliver it to you, but my heart cried 'coward,' and I knew I owed you the respect of delivering it myself. I regret that I am unable to relieve you of your suffering as you have relieved the suffering of my men."

A bell dinged loudly out in the harbor, drawing their attention. The soldier near the horses called to the general.

"Sir, you may want to come see this!"

Together, they followed the general out the door and into the yard.

"There," pointed the soldier.

In the harbor, the last British ship had sailed away from the dock and was making its way towards the open ocean. Its white sails billowed in the wind, its flag flapping proudly in the breeze.

The general sighed. "This is only the beginning. They will return, and with the king's temper."

They watched until the ship had all but faded from view.

"Mercy, I promise to make good on that debt," the general said.

"How?" asked Mercy.

"We are going to win the war," General Washington answered.

Glossary
of Uncommon or Difficult Words

Ambush: A surprise attack, often along a road.

Apprehensively: Nervously, timidly, with reservation.

Artillery: Cannons and mortars.

Banter: Playful teasing remarks.

Buckboard: The driver's seat of a wagon.

Cache: Hidden stockpile.

Cadence: A rhythmic song, chant, or beat.

Continentals: American regular army soldiers.

Coywolf: Coyote, smaller wolflike wild canine.

Dumbfounded: At a loss for words, speechless, unable to comprehend.

Duress: Under threat or force, compelled forcibly.

Exponentially: A multiplied rate of growth.

Fortifications: Defenses, walls, fences, forts, towers, etc.

Gallivanting: Going about in a pleasurable but frivolous manner.

Garrison: Military fort.

Grapples: Three-pronged iron hooks at the end of ropes.

Incessant: Nonstop.

Militia: Volunteer military units called upon from a common geographical area.

Mortars: Short stubby cannons that launched larger, often explosive, cannonballs.

Mundane: Boring, dull.

Munitions: Ammunition, powder, musket balls, cannonballs, etc.

Patriot: Someone who voluntarily fights for their country believing it is their duty to do so.

Redcoat: British regular soldier.

Regulars: British enlisted soldiers.

Rudimentary: Crude, unrefined, basic.

Ruse: Fake, a trick.

Shot: Tiny lead pellets used for hunting birds and small game with a musket.

Subjugate: Make someone a slave.

Tory: An individual loyal to the British Crown.

Volley: An orderly singular discharge of weapons from a line of soldiers or artillery by command.

Whimsical: Carefree, unpredictable, fanciful.

It's not over yet!

I'd love to help other readers enjoy this book as much as you have. If you'd just take a minute and let them know your favorite scene, how the story impacted you, or what book or author you'd compare it to, it will help other readers find it. It's your best way to show your support for us and we greatly appreciate it!

Just scan this QR code to get to the Amazon review page and leave your review!

(Even if you purchased or received this copy from somewhere else, you're still eligible to leave a review on Amazon if you have an active account.)

Get your FREE Gifts from J. E. Ribbey!

FREE Story Quiz for The Innocent Rebel
With a separate answer key!

FREE Printable Map
including Lexington, Cambridge, Boston, and Dorchester Heights!

To get these FREE resources and to find out what happens next to Mercy and her family, scan the QR code or visit our website at JERibbey.com!

Scan Me

About the Author

J.E. Ribbey, a husband & wife team, deploys a compelling writing style, combining a fast-paced action thriller with deep character immersion, giving readers an edge-of-your-seat adventure they will feel in the morning. A combat veteran, outdoorsman, and survival enthusiast, Joel enjoys mingling his unique experiences and expertise with his passion for homesteading and the self-sufficient lifestyle in his writing. A homeschooling mom, homesteader, and digital designer, Esther brings the technical, editorial, and design skills to the author team. Together with their four kids they manage a small farmstead in Minnesota, where, besides taking care of the animals and gardens, they also run an event venue and small campground. If you'd like to know more, you can find the Ribbeys on Instagram @j.e.ribbey or at their website JERibbey.com.

Made in United States
Cleveland, OH
16 March 2025